MY TYPE ON PAPER

MY TYPE ON PAPER

SCHOLASTIC

Chloe Seager

Scholastic Children's Books
An imprint of Scholastic Ltd
Euston House, 24 Eversholt Street, London, NW1 1DB, UK
Registered office: Westfield Road, Southam, Warwickshire, CV47 0RA
SCHOLASTIC and associated logos are trademarks and/or
registered trademarks of Scholastic Inc.

First published in the UK by Scholastic Ltd, 2020

Text copyright © Chloe Seager, 2020

The right of Chloe Seager to be identified as the
author of this work has been asserted by her.

ISBN 978 0 702 30209 1

A CIP catalogue record for this book
is available from the British Library.

Printed by CPI Group (UK) Ltd, Croydon, CR0 4YY
Papers used by Scholastic Children's Books are made
from wood grown in sustainable forests.

1 3 5 7 9 10 8 6 4 2

This is a work of fiction. Names, characters, places, incidents
and dialogues are products of the author's imagination or are used
fictitiously. Any resemblance to actual people, living or dead,
events or locales is entirely coincidental.

www.scholastic.co.uk

CHAPTER

ONE

So this is what heartbreak feels like.

According to the songs, lightning will strike me down or my legs will give way beneath me or my lungs will physically stop taking oxygen in and out *any moment now.*

Wait for it. . .

Nope, I'm still here. Breathing, blinking, craving Jaffa cakes. I wish lightning *would* strike me. The pain of death surely cannot be worse than this.

I look at the message again.

Sorry M. It's clear we both know it's best to end things here. x

That's the bit I'm really struggling with. "We both know it's best." *Do we???!!* I don't *think* I know it's for the best. What *I think* I know is best is for us to still be together, and for me to be going on his family holiday as planned. That's right. *Family holiday.* And not just any family holiday ... a holiday in a massive villa with an infinity pool. I mean, talk about incredible?! Who even has an infinity pool, apart from people in films and apparently Freddie and his family? It's all very glamorous. Well ... it *was* going to be glamorous. How, last week, were we at the "family holiday" stage of our relationship, and now we're at the "let's end things here" stage?!

Does "ending" even count as a stage? And was I really giving off the vibes I wanted to end things? Am I allowed to argue with a message that tells me what I think? "Um no, sorry, I think you've got it wrong." Or am I the one who has it wrong? *Do* I know it's best we end things, but I just don't know I know?! Was I, actually, the one to subconsciously break up with *him*?!

In all the songs, no one ever warned me heartbreak could be so *confusing*.

Dad knocks on my door. My trampled heart sinks. Dad is perplexed when I well up during adopt-a-donkey adverts, so I dread to think how he'll react to my "boy problems".

"Maya, how's packing going?"

"Uh..." I glance over at the suitcase beside my bed. My tops are neatly folded next to my shorts, laid on top of my dresses, which are spread at the bottom of the case to give them more room. My bikinis sit next to my new range of thermal underwear and a carefully chosen selection of books lines the zip section. I've been packed for days, a) because I'm hyper-organized and b) because up until ten minutes ago I was really, *really* excited about this trip.

"Have you remembered your thermal undies?" Dad laughs.

"Yes, Dad," I call through gritted teeth.

Great. Not only did I buy thermal underwear for nothing, I had *multiple conversations with my Dad about thermal underwear* for nothing.

"I hear Spain is freezing this time of year," he laughs for the millionth time. You know you've really hit rock bottom when even your own parent is mocking you. But when Freddie said we would be camping a couple of nights, it seemed sensible to invest in some warm under-gear ... even if we *were* going to Spain mostly to lie around in a pool.

"You must be getting excited now!" I can hear Dad clicking his fingers and jumping outside my bedroom door. "*Olé!*"

"Yep, I can barely contain myself," I call back flatly.

"All right, well, I'll leave you to it." Dad retreats from my door.

Urghhhhhhhhhhhhhhhhhhhh. How am I going to explain this to Dad?! He's going to be heartbroken for me, which is even worse than me being heartbroken. He flaps around like a panicked chicken when I lose a glove or . . . stub a toe, let alone get dumped! (If I did, in actual fact, get dumped, and didn't subconsciously will my own relationship's demise.)

My phone buzzes again. It's Aimee.

URM, so I heard you and Freddie are no more?

How do you know that?? It happened TEN MINUTES ago! I write back.

Don't worry, everyone knows, she says.

Oh, great. What a comfort. She starts typing again.

Freddie told Lydia and you know she's got a huge mouth. The big question is, what are you going to do with that massive pile of thermal underwear?

The antithesis of my dad, my best friend Aimee is *brutal*. She says that's how a) I know she loves me, because you can only be rude to the people you really love, and b) that's how I know everything is actually OK. Because if she was being nice to me, something truly terrible must have happened.

I'm on my way over, she says. **Joe is here so he's coming too.**

Joe is our other best mate. He and Aimee spend a lot of time playing video games together that I neither understand nor want to understand. It used to be just me and Aimee, but then Aimee met Joe at some gaming event and said he was the only boy there who "took her seriously" *before* she beat them all. They instantly hit it off and it turned out he actually went to our school, we'd just never noticed him. Joe is one of those boys who isn't popular, or unpopular, he just sort of slides under the radar. But once Aimee and I spotted him, we wondered why we never did before.

I spend the next ten minutes wailing into a pillow. When I hear Joe and Aimee ring the doorbell I try to cry in a more attractive and ladylike manner, and put my sunglasses on to hide my giant, puffy eyes. Then I remember my already perfectly packed suitcase, which Aimee will definitely mock me for, so I run to shove it under the bed. *Then* I remember the "My Dream Holiday Romance" quiz in my magazine that I filled out six different times trying to get to the boy most similar to Freddie, which is all covered in doodles of hearts and "*Maya <3 Freddie*" and "*we found love (in a cloudless place...)*"

I manage to close it and fling myself back on to the bed as they open my bedroom door.

"Sorry you're upset, Maya," Joe says as he enters. "I moved a snail from the pavement in your honour, so it wouldn't get trodden on."

"And I brought snacks," says Aimee, holding out a giant box of Jaffa cakes. Aimee knows me so well.

I'd been lying on my back with my hand resting against my forehead, sort of because it's comfortable and sort of because, if I *did* die of heartbreak as the songs suggested, I would look deeply tragic and poetic when they walked in the room. But the Jaffa cakes tempt me out of my Juliet-like position. I sit up, eyes on the box.

"Wow, snail rescue and snacks, I don't know what to say." My voice wobbles. Aimee's coming dangerously close to being nice to me. Things must be bad.

"You look like a moron." She points at my sunglasses.

OK, so not that bad.

Joe perches on the edge of my bed, hiding slightly under his curls. Although we've all been friends for years now, he never looks *quite* at home in mine and Aimee's bedrooms. Aimee, however, settles right in and leaps on to my bed, ripping open the Jaffa cakes. She shoves one in her mouth and one towards me. Then, suddenly, she looks like she might vomit.

"Oh God, you've PACKED," she shouts through a mouthful of cake. Crumbs fly everywhere. She points at the corner of my suitcase, poking out from under the bed. *Oh My Days.* I didn't do a very good job of hiding it. Note to self: never attempt a career as a spy.

"Of course I packed," I answer, as if I wasn't trying to hide the suitcase. "I don't leave things until eleven p.m. the night before like *some people*, Aimee."

Joe nods in agreement.

Aimee looks between me and Joe. "You mean like *normal people*."

She leaps up and starts heaving the suitcase out from under my bed.

"Oh my god, Maya, what have you got in here? Supplies for the zombie apocalypse?!"

"*Stop it!!!*" I cry, hitting her with my sunglasses. "Hey! Put it back!"

I'm not ready. If I leave my suitcase where it is, I can pretend I am still going on my perfect holiday with my perfect boyfriend.

"Nope," Aimee replies, flinging it open. "Because otherwise you're going to spend all week staring at it."

"*Am not!!*" I whine.

"Oh, you so are," says Aimee.

"I'm not. I'm going to unpack tomorrow morning, promise. I have a careful system. . ."

But Aimee is already flinging clothes left, right and centre. A pair of thermal pants hit Joe in the face. He blushes and pretends not to notice what they are.

One minute later my room is *covered in clothes.*

"Great, now I'm alone *and* messy!" I wail, looking around in dismay.

"You're welcome." Aimee bows. She puts one pair of thermal pants on over her jeans and another pair on her head, then sits back on the bed.

We all sit in silence for a moment. She looks ridiculous.

"Anyway, you're not alone." Aimee starts again. "You've got me and Joe." Joe nods and smiles at this. "And who wants to spend a summer in *Spain,* when you could be in the *United Kingdom*?" Bless her for trying, but if she thinks calling the UK the "United Kingdom" is going to make it sound glamorous and majestic, she is mistaken.

I raise one eyebrow. Joe coughs. "Er, I want to be supportive, but ... I'm kind of with Maya on this one," he says.

"Check the weather, pals." Aimee folds her arms smugly. "They're saying it's going to be the hottest summer on record."

"I'll believe that when I see it." I roll my eyes. "Now I'll never get to flamenco dance!"

Aimee snorts. "No offence, but I don't think you would have been a natural."

"I could have learned!"

"Yeah," Aimee snorts. "Just like you learned netball, or karate, or—"

"All right, *thanks*, Aimee. I guess I'll never discover any of my *probably loads of hidden talents* with you around. You're so encouraging."

It was true; I wasn't the most physically gifted person. My talents lie more *in the mind*. Still, flamenco could have been my thing. I'll never know now, will I?!

Joe, who had been carefully deconstructing a Jaffa cake this entire time so that he could eat each section separately, finally chimes in. "To be honest, M, I'm not sure Freddie would have gone with you anyway. We can go if you like?"

"Thanks, Joe." I try to sound sincere. But obviously, this is not really about my latent potential as a world-class flamenco dancer.

"Oh my God," Aimee says.

No, no, no. She's spied the magazine. She reaches for it just as I lunge, but she's faster than me. I topple off the bed in a heap.

"My Dream Summer Romance," she reads out. "Maya, what *is* this??" she shrieks.

I cringe.

"What's your dream boy's job? Oh, look what Maya's put ... *comedian.* That's funny, because I thought you wanted to be a doctor. Doctor and comedian don't seem like an *obvious choice* to me..."

"I don't have to date another doctor!" I yell.

Aimee ignores me. "Didn't Freddie want to do stand-up, Joe? Even though, let's face it, I've met cats that are wittier."

Joe fixates even harder on his deconstructed Jaffa cake.

"What is the most important attribute to you? *Disorganized.* Oh my God! Don't make me laugh!"

Joe shrugs, still staring at the Jaffa cake.

"Opposites attract!" I shake my fist at her.

"What is your..."

"All right, I get it, I'm a sad case!" I cry. "Why are you torturing me?!"

"I just think you've always been weirdly fixated on Freddie, and he *ain't all that*, and there are plenty of fish in the sea."

I sniff. Aimee never liked Freddie much. And all right, we weren't the kind of couple you'd expect to see going out... He hung around with people like Lydia McKenzie. People who have never tripped over their own feet and always seem to be *having lives* on social media. But the girls' magazine gods, in their infinite wisdom, had spoken. We were *destined* to be together.

Aimee realizes she's gone too far when I reach for the sunglasses again.

"Sorry, M." She pats me on the head. "But maybe he just wasn't as perfect as you thought. Shall we fill out the quiz a different way? Would that cheer you up? Look at all these other answers you put before crossing them out and ending up with the magazine clone of Freddie!" She puts on a big, fake grin. Even Joe nods vigorously, as if filling out a lame quiz in a girlie magazine is the most unimaginably exciting thing he can think of doing.

They're sweet, but I don't want anyone else except Freddie. Even in a stupid, imaginary quiz-world. I'd met my perfect match, age sixteen, and now he's gone I might as well join a convent.

"I don't want another dream summer romance," I say. "I can't conceive of anyone who ticks more of my boxes. Freddie's my type down to a T." And OK, so he likes being the centre of attention whereas I make a *great* audience member, and he always forgets to do his homework whereas I've sometimes done it before it's even been set, but that was what worked... I mean, I'd laugh at his jokes and help with his homework. We *complemented each other.*

Aimee shakes her head. "Sorry, Maya, but you need a new type. Freddie's muggy as."

"Freddie's not *muggy*!" I defend.

Aimee says nothing, just points at her mug of tea.

"Look on the bright side," she continues. "At least now you don't have to spend any more time with Lydia McKenzie."

I nod but my stomach clenches. I would never admit this to Aimee but ... well ... I didn't mind spending time with Lydia. She was actually really nice and, OMD, she knows how to do a perfect smize.

"I just..." I begin. "I just... I just thought..."

"You were going to declare your undying love under the Spanish sun, gazing into each other's eyes across a juicy paella, giggling as you rolled around in the sand?"

"Well, yes, pretty much," I admit.

Aimee sighs. "Well, guess what, he PIED YOU OVER TEXT. So, *THANK U, NEXT.*"

Aimee has such a way with words. Joe presses his lips together and says more softly, "She's probably right, M."

I give a small nod, even though I don't agree. There's no point arguing with Aimee. We spend the next hour hanging out, watching stupid shows on Netflix. It's nearly eight by the time I wave them off. I feel a bit better whilst they're here, but as soon as they're gone this horrible, empty feeling settles back in my stomach. (Which is surprising given how full of Jaffa cakes it is).

I *know* Aimee's right. *Thank u, next,* and all that. I want to feel that way, I do. But I can't help it. . . I'm just not like her. (*Or* Ariana.) Aimee meets people easily. I lose track of the number of guys she dates and when things end she doesn't seem to mind. She's usually the one ending them. I haven't really dated anybody else. . . Freddie is it. And I really thought Freddie was *it*.

He made everyone laugh, and even though he didn't necessarily care about schoolwork he didn't need to because he was probably going to be a famous stand-up one day. He was tall-but-not-too-tall, he had *dimples* on each cheek and well-proportioned elbows, and he limited his meat intake to help the environment even though he *really* loved bacon, and he always ate all his peas. The five million personality tests I did all said we were the ideal match. The fourteen bajillion "is-he-the-one" quizzes I filled out all said we were *definitely going to be together for ever.* You know, on the sixth go at least (no one gets the correct result the first time they take those quizzes, do they?)

Where did I go wrong?!?!

CHAPTER

 TWO

It's a new dawn, it's a new day, and I'm feeling *much* better than I did yesterday. Have I accepted my dream relationship's end with my one true soulmate and moved on already? Well, no, not quite.

The more I think about it, the more I think there *must* have been some horrible mistake. Otherwise he wouldn't have said, "We both know it's best." Clearly, I have put out some kind of signal that I also wanted things to end and, after spending most of the night going over *every single moment of the last two weeks* and holding it under a microscope in my mind, I *think* I know where it happened... It was probably when he offered me his spare cap and I said not to worry, because I'd already bought myself a hat with an umbrella attached. (I was delighted to discover these are a real thing! And you can use them in rain or shine!) Freddie said, "You're kidding," and I said, "I was surprised too, but look! Isn't it highly practical *and* fun?" He looked at the hat and then went a bit silent, so I probably really hurt his feelings by rejecting his offer. He probably wanted to do that cute "matching couple" thing.

Last night at one a.m. I finally replied to his message, and said:

> **I'm sorry if it came across like I wanted things to end. I didn't. I'll wear your cap if you want? I just thought the umbrella hat was rather snazzy. X**

He hasn't replied yet but I'm hoping this will fix things.

My phone buzzes and my heart leaps into my throat. Sadly, it's only Joe.

> **Hey, just warning you Aimee is plotting something to help with the Freddie situation. Not sure what but wanted you to be prepared. X**

Oh my days... What is she up to?? It doesn't take

long to find out. My phone buzzes again five minutes later and Aimee's face appears on my screen.

"Maya, you are going to *love* me."

"What have you done?" I ask.

"There's no need to sound so afraid." She rolls her eyes. "I haven't knocked Freddie unconscious and tied him up in my basement." She pauses, before making her big announcement. "I got you a summer job!"

I open my mouth to respond but no words come out. When I don't reply, she carries on.

"With me and Joe! *At Casa Nadar!*" she cries.

My heart melts into a puddle. This is *so* nice I want to cry. Joe and Aimee were going to work at our local outdoor pool as lifeguards all summer, whilst I was meant to be sitting in the sun with Freddie and his family. We all did lifeguard training last year so we're all technically qualified. But those jobs filled up *super quickly* at the beginning of summer.

Casa Nadar wasn't always called Casa Nadar. Up until a few months ago it was called "Bayside Swim Centre". Thanks to a huge amount of investment money from a snazzy out-of-town corporation it had a big makeover a few months ago and became less like a local community pool, and more like a glamorous movie set with a fake beach and sunloungers. Lifeguarding there is one of those jobs everyone wants because, provided no one drowns, you don't do much except sipping smoothies and hanging out with your friends in the sun.

"Aimee…" I start. "That's so nice of you. I know you probably pulled loads of strings and…" I gulp. "But I wish you'd spoken to me first. I think everything's actually going to be OK with Freddie."

"OH!" She tries not to sound too surprised. "What happened? Did he come grovelling? Are you guys back together, then?"

"Umm, well, no, not *exactly*… Well, it's more that I realized this is probably all a silly misunderstanding."

There's a silence.

"About a hat."

More silence. I carry on.

"So once we've cleared things up I'm sure we'll be back together and I'll be going on the trip as planned."

"Right, OK, M," Aimee says finally. "Cool, cool. Look, I'm just going to leave the job offer hanging until the end of the day, all right? No rush, just … let me know by seven."

She doesn't believe me! I can't *believe* she doesn't believe me! Aimee never says "cool, cool" unless she thinks someone is talking utter rubbish!

"I don't *need* until seven," I say through gritted teeth. "I told you, I'm going *on holiday*. Freddie and I are getting back together and the summer is going to be absolutely perfect."

"Yeah, I heard you, cool cool," Aimee says unconvincingly. "OK. Well, even so, just think about it, all right?"

"I told you, I don't need. . ."

But her face disappears from my screen. That girl can be so stubborn when she's wrong.

But by four, having spent the day staring at my phone and willing it to buzz, I can't deny that a chink of doubt is starting to appear in my mind. Freddie *always* has his phone on him. He was pretty much always messaging his mates when we were together. (He's *such* a good friend.) He must have seen it by now? Unless he's so hurt by our break-up he can't bear to speak to anyone?

I bet that's it. I must have hurt him really bad, with my false subliminal break-up messages and hat rejection.

At quarter to six, when I've about given up all hope and am lying, once again, on my bed with my hand across my forehead and my sunglasses on, Dad calls that dinner is nearly ready. I contemplate staying in my room for ever and starving myself, and Freddie will see "local girl too heartbroken to eat again" on the news and then he will *have* to invite me to Spain. But Dad's an *interesting* cook. (Another thing on my perfect boyfriend checklist: cooking. Freddie made me a sandwich once and got the proportion of mayo to bread *just right*. Another sign he's perfect for me.) I usually have to intervene to avoid disaster, so I put my hunger strike on hold and go downstairs.

Plus, given that I haven't heard from Freddie, I should probably break it to Dad that I'm no longer going away. *Gulp.* I still haven't had the nerve to tell him, partly because I can't face up to his disappointment and partly because I was still hoping Freddie would change his mind.

When Dad's cooking it tends to look like a bomb has hit the kitchen. There are pots and pans and herbs scattered around the surfaces. Much like Aimee, he has no respect for my organizational skills. I arranged the herb cupboard *yesterday*. (Still, now I'm definitely not going to Spain I suppose I've got all the time in the world to reorganize it).

"What are you making, Dad?" I ask.

"A risotto. . ." He starts. He sounds far away. "I made it with your mum once. But, I don't know. Something's not right. . ." He grabs another pot of herbs and pinches some between his fingers. "No." He shakes his head. Then he reaches for some cinnamon.

"It's not going to be cinnamon..." I say, before he starts shaking it in the pan.

He stirs, leans in and inhales. Then he tastes a little bit on a wooden spoon.

"No, you're right," he says. "Not cinnamon. Oh well, hope you're OK with bizarre Christmassy risotto tonight."

This is what I mean about Dad's cooking. He's brilliant when I make sure the right ingredients are to hand and I'm around to stop him lobbing anything in that he can get his hands on.

We sit down and he fills me in about his day, and I realize I've been so wrapped up in my misery that I've barely seen him. I feel guilty for burying myself up in my room all weekend and eat my strange-tasting risotto without pulling a face.

When we're finished eating he says, "Not my best. Still, never know when you're going to chance on that missing ingredient that completes the dish, and makes it amazing." He kisses his fingers. "So, you excited for tomorrow?"

I open my mouth. Here is my moment. It's coming... *I'm going to tell him.*

But what if Freddie has replied?

I nod and run back upstairs. I left my phone in my room and haven't looked at it all the way through dinner, so maybe... Maybe I'll hear from Freddie and everything will be on again, and I won't have to tell Dad at all. And everything will be perfect and…

Yes!!! There is a message!! My heart leaps and I pounce on it, desperate to hear that this was all a big misunderstanding.

Only, it still isn't Freddie.

It's Lydia McKenzie.

I double-take at the unfamiliar sight of her name on my phone screen. Lydia's always been really nice to me because she's Freddie's friend, but we don't often message each other. Is she getting in touch to say how sorry she is to hear about the break-up?! Oh, that's so *sweet* of her. I knew Aimee was wrong about her! I always said she was a good egg.

Then I read the message.

Hi Maya. I just wanted to send a quick one to make sure there's no awkwardness about me going to Spain with Freddie! Lots of love, L xxx

It's like my heart is the *Titanic* colliding with a giant, unanticipated iceberg. I blink at the screen as tears start to prickle my eyes. *Lydia?* He's *invited Lydia on his family holiday*, less than twenty-four hours after we broke up? Is this some kind of mistake?! This can't be right.

I just sit on my bed for ages, staring into space and absorbing this unexpected information. But why would she say it if it wasn't true? No ... it must be. I look at Lydia's message again and burst into tears. Will I ever stop crying, I wonder? Is this it now? Is this what I do?! Cry?!?! The sad thing is that it's *biologically impossible* to run out of tears unless you have an associated medical condition. I literally could *keep crying for ever.*

Is he with Lydia now? Are they going to make it official looking out over the beautiful, romantic sunset that I was supposed to see?! But ... but ... Lydia and Freddie don't belong. *Me and Freddie* belong. Lydia won't help Freddie with his homework, or remind him what books he needs for certain lessons. And she's always in the limelight herself ... they'd be constantly battling for it. It would be a *complete disaster.*

I think sadly about how Freddie and I got together. I'd had a crush on him for ages, after analysing all the boys in our year and concluding he was the obvious choice (due to aforementioned height and other appearance factors, ability to make others laugh and natural aptitude for sciences, despite not yet reaching full potential due to lack of organization). I'd observed that Freddie was *always* late to class, so in our first biology lesson of the new year I sat with Joe until everyone else had taken their seats, then made Joe move at the very last minute (to sit next to Ronald Smith, a mouth-breather who no one wants to sit with, sorry, Joe). By the time Freddie arrived, the seat next to me was the *only available one*. He laughed at my joke about mitosis (I said it was proving to be a "divisive issue") and said I was so clever he'd be honoured to learn from me. (I suppose one of the best ways to learn is copying someone else's answers). And it was all *anaerobic respiration* from there. (Get it? Taking each other's breath away?)

Why would he end a relationship with that calibre of science-related in-jokes?

Except . . . except . . . as I look at a picture of Freddie and Lydia on Freddie's Instagram, from a few weeks ago, I can't help but think how good they look together.

I wipe a tear from my eye. Maybe I've been kidding myself. Maybe opposites *don't* attract. Maybe shiny people like Lydia and Freddie do belong together on fabulous Spanish vacations, whether she's going with him romantically *or* just as a friend, and people like me belong at home in the UK studying mitosis in their bedroom.

Eventually I shake myself and force my eyes to stop watering. That, surely, is enough toxins and stress hormones released. Good luck to them, I say. I bet Lydia doesn't have a super-cool umbrella hat. *May they both be cursed to walk in the shade.*

If there's anything I hate, it's not knowing where I'm headed, and the last couple of days I've let myself spiral uncharacteristically out of control. It's time to pull myself together. I finally march downstairs and tell Dad I'm not going away. In typical Daddish fashion, he looks painfully concerned but thankfully doesn't ask any questions. Before he can ask me if I'm OK, I march back upstairs, because if I talk about it I might cry yet again. Taking a deep breath, I message Aimee.

You were right. Still have room for me at the pool?

She replies quickly.

I didn't want to be right. Always have room for you. Ax

I'm feeling a bit better already. What I need is a plan. *A new plan.* I'd spent so long looking forward to this holiday with Freddie that it was hard to imagine my summer going any other way. But thanks to Aimee I've already got a new job. I rack my brains. What else can

I do to reclaim my summer? Dye my hair an outlandish colour that in no way complements my skin tone? Get some sort of ill-advised piercing?

Am I going to sign up to a *gym?!*

I'm just thinking through all these terrifying plans when I see my magazine lying in the bin. Aha! I snatch it and open it up to the "Dream Summer Romance" quiz, where I'd tried so hard to get the Freddie-clone that I felt sure was my destiny. I look down at my scribbling mess of answers and realize, for the first time, I'm not so sure any more.

I think about what Aimee said about opening my mind to new kinds of people. Well, actually, that's not strictly what she said. I think she said, "Thank u, next," and that I needed a new type because "Freddie is muggy". For the first time I wonder if she's right. I've definitely never *heard* of soulmates pieing each other off via text message.

I look back through the answers I selected and then disregarded, because Freddie was none of those things. I grab a pencil, scribble out my Freddie result, and start again. It feels weird. As if Freddie, wherever he is right now, can feel me crossing him out. . .

Question 1: What's your dream
guy's job?

a. Doctor
b. Vet
c. Actor
d. Musician
e. Comedian
f. Banker
g. App-developer
h. Surfer
i. Fireman
j. Pilot

Instead of putting "comedian" I put "vet", which was
my first instinct. Not a "doctor", like I want to be, but
similar enough that we would probably share values.
Which leads me on to. . .

Question 2: What is the most
important attribute to you?

a. Conscientious
b. Sensitive
c. Passionate

d. Humorous
e. Ambitious
f. Loyal
g. Free-spirited
h. Creative
i. Adventurous
j. Athletic

This time I give "humorous" a miss. And I figure if this boy's a vet he's already conscientious, so I'd quite like him to be "sensitive" as well.

I keep answering the questions until I build a dreamy summer romance with a caring, animal-loving, aspiring young vet spending a summer dog-sitting for his aunt, who even has a little scar on his arm from falling out of a tree rescuing a kitten.

I had sometimes wondered what it would be like to be with a "sensitive" guy. I'm *highly sensitive* so I'd always told myself Freddie would balance me out. But maybe I would like to date a more thoughtful person? At least, a "sensitive" guy surely wouldn't break up with me by text.

This is actually fun. I go again, excited by the prospect that there could be other kinds of people out there for me. If Freddie isn't my type after all, then I have to find out who *is!*

Question 1: What's your dream guy's job?

This time I put "surfer" because, *ahem*, why not.

Question 2: What is the most important attribute to you?

This time I go a bit wild and choose "free-spirited." By the time I get to the bottom again, I've got myself a summer romance with a built, action-man type, taking a relaxing week out of a whirlwind backpacking tour of Europe and "riding the waves" to teach swimming. I'd never seen myself with one of those guys because ... well ... I liked Freddie's body type (slim) so assumed I couldn't like any others. But, I admit, sometimes when I see really ripped guys coming out of the gym *I blush*. An undeniable sign of physical attraction.

Freddie always used to say people who "went travelling" lacked direction. He only ever wanted to go away to his family's house in Spain. I agreed with him at the time, but now that I think about it, a drive to see the world and live in the moment... Perhaps I would enjoy spending time with someone who was more of a "seize the day" type?

More men, please!

Question 1: What's your dream
guy's job?

This time I put "musician."

Question 2: What is the most
important attribute to you?

This time I choose "ambitious."

At the school talent contest this year I obviously only had
eyes for Freddie, who did a stand-up set, but I have to
admit, the band who were on after him were *quite sexy*.

I've always found ambition attractive. Freddie has
goals, obviously, but … I don't know. He had goals but
never seemed to actually *do* anything towards them?
Like, for someone like Freddie, he just sort of expects
things will fall in his lap. And maybe they will. But
maybe I'd quite like to go out with someone who will
stop at nothing to get what he wants in life, and won't
let anything stand in his way. Now that sounds like
taking planning to the next level. Who wouldn't want
to be inspired by their partner? We could set each other

measurable career goals and reward each other with snogs when we reached them.

This time I end up with an edgy singer and guitarist, with a super-cool haircut and fashionable DMs, following his ambition to become a musician by gigging all summer long.

I look back at all three guys I've designed for myself and *swoon*. Even though they're only on paper, at this moment they feel more real to me than Freddie, who's probably packing for his flight tomorrow without me.

It's getting late and Dad finally shouts at me to turn out my light, so I put the quiz to one side, and fall asleep dreaming of vets, surfers and musicians ... and *most definitely not* about Freddie.

CHAPTER

THREE

I didn't fall asleep thinking about Freddie, but I did dream about him. He was on a surfboard, wearing nothing but speedos and DMs and holding a puppy, chasing me around my house. It was quite odd. I try not to think about it as I get changed into my new "Casa Nadar" uniform, which Aimee (bless her) dropped round my house before she went in to work.

I was hoping I'd feel better this morning, but whatever spell of Beyoncé-type empowerment I was under last night seems to have faded with the rising sun. Earlier I messaged Lydia to say, *"No hard feelings, have a nice time xx"* and I thought it would make me feel magnanimous and mature, but all it did was make me feel even more like dog poo.

When I step outside I'm hit by a wall of heat. It's *boiling*. There's not a cloud in sight and the sky is so blue it looks like an Instagram photo where someone's turned the saturation up unrealistically high. Except it *is* real. I guess Aimee was right about this being the hottest summer ever. Well, at least the ten bottles of factor fifty I bought to take to Spain won't be completely wasted.

Casa Nadar is about a ten-minute walk from my house. It's a big, square building with giant windows and has been painted white in the makeover. It looks so out of place in between all the other buildings, it feels like it should be sitting somewhere in the Spanish countryside rather than the UK. If I squint and ignore the rest of the street, I could *almost* pretend I was on holiday with Freddie right now.

There's an indoor pool, visible through the huge floor-to-ceiling windows, and a huge new outdoor pool (it must be nearly Olympic-sized, surely?!) with three different diving boards; the tallest one looks frighteningly high. Running around the water is wooden decking, lined with sunloungers and tables, and behind that an expanse of grass and strategically placed flowers. On the opposite side there's an actual beach (how long did it take them to get all that imported sand in place?!) with not only more sunloungers, but one of those four-poster luxury sunbeds that famous people and royals sit on. The whole place is marked off from the streets with pretty iron gates like it's a palace.

I stop just outside the gates. I've heard a lot of talk about it at school, but didn't really listen because I wasn't going to be here. Plus I assumed everyone was exaggerating. But the new pearly white Casa Nadar, combined with the blazing hot weather, does actually look idyllic.

When I get inside Aimee's waiting for me. She's in her uniform and obviously pulling it off much better than I will. Aimee's very petite and curvy, with a graceful dancer's body, whereas I'm quite tall and awkward-limbed and distinctly un-curvy, so clothes hang off me weirdly. Aimee says I'm "model-like", but I'm not sure I trust her for an accurate measure of my true attractiveness. She once said I looked nice in flares.

"How's it going, M?" She holds her arms out and gestures behind her to Casa Nadar. "See, who needs Freddie when you've got all of this?"

I give her a weak smile. It's undeniably gorgeous, but I still feel awful about my cancelled holiday.

"Babe, I swear, by the end of the day you'll forget all about Freddie," Aimee promises. "There's going to be *loads* of fit guys here."

She says this just as Mr Wallace, our decidedly unfit and extremely hairy English teacher, walks past.

"Morning, girls," he says with a salute. "Just clearing out the pipes with a glorious morning swim."

I wait until he passes then raise my eyebrow at her.

"All the fit ones come later," she says.

We both burst out laughing. I'm just starting to think maybe Aimee's right, maybe the summer will actually be sun-soaked and laughter-filled and Aimee, Joe and I can just chill out and enjoy being in this beautiful palace, when I see *Belinda Belmont*.

Nooooo.

And she's coming towards me.

Nooooooooo.

Why is she coming towards me?!

Belinda is a couple of years above us at school. She already completed college so I thought I'd never have to see her again, but clearly that was a pipe dream. Belinda was the school netball captain (and captain of pretty much every sports team you can think of). A few years ago Aimee convinced me that signing up for netball would be "fun". I stupidly listened to her and came to the try-outs, only to be given a pity place on the subs bench. That would have been fine, if useless Anthea Manning hadn't *broken her ankle* before the inter-school championships, meaning I had to actually play as goal-shooter.

Thankfully, the goal attack was good enough that the ball hardly ever came my way. The person marking me stopped bothering halfway through the game. But then came the crucial moment. We were nearly at the end of the game, it was four-all, the ball was our end, our goal attack was being marked by two players. Centre was looking for someone to pass to, anyone but me... But, alas, I was the only choice. I caught the ball and then got so excited about catching the ball, I ran with it at top speed to the goalpost. The goalpost loomed... I threw it... And...

IT WENT IN!

The only thing is, you're not supposed to run with the ball in netball. Apparently that's, like, important. The goal was disqualified and the other team regained possession, scored last-minute and won.

I will never forgive Anthea Manning. Or her weak ankles.

Belinda will never forgive me.

She moves closer to us (chest first, as usual – Belinda has *fantastic* boobs. To be fair, if I had boobs like that I'd probably draw attention to them as well). I look at Aimee. Aimee looks back. She sees the confusion and fear in my eyes and says, "Look, M..."

But as Belinda approaches I understand. She's wearing the Casa Nadar uniform too and she has a clipboard and a little cap. She's the *manager*. Of course she is. Belinda never liked me much, but she *loves* Aimee, who is an integral part of half the school's sports teams. It's now making way more sense how she swung me this job.

"Oh. . ." I falter. "Good to see you, Belinda. Are you having a nice summer?"

Belinda blinks at me. She never was one for small talk.

"For you." She raises one perfectly plucked eyebrow and brandishes a mop.

I stare at the mop for a second. "Oh, I think there's been a misunderstanding," I say. "I'm here as another lifeguard."

Belinda blinks again. Slowly, like a lizard. She puts one hand on her hip and pushes her bum out (another fantastic feature of Belinda's that she likes to show off).

"No misunderstanding." She smiles falsely. "I told Ames that it was this or nothing." She holds the mop closer to me.

Ames?

Suddenly it dawns on me. I'm not here as a lifeguard. . . I'm here as a *cleaner!* I don't believe it! Is this *genuinely happening?* One minute I'm supposed to be going on a fabulous holiday with my dreamy boyfriend, and the next I'm *scrubbing toilets?!*

I glare at Aimee, who looks like she's trying to disappear into the shadows. There's only so long I can stand here open-mouthed. Reluctantly, I take the mop. Belinda's smug smile spreads wider across her face. She's enjoying this *way too much*.

"Excellent, well, now that's all *cleared up.*" She chuckles menacingly. "You can do the toilets."

Then she prances out of the room, swishing her long ponytail. I turn my head sharply to Aimee, who has her hands pressed together pleadingly. "Look, don't get mad. I knew if I told you, you'd say no. And it's *much* better that you're here, rather than moping around in your room all summer. If you think about it, it's a relatively small price to pay to hang out with me."

"You rate yourself highly," I say flatly.

"Yeah, I do." She flicks her hair. "Now, off you go. I've got lives to save and you've got urine to wipe."

I didn't think it was possible, but my summer *actually just got worse.*

Ten minutes later I'm already planning how to hand in my notice to Belinda. How bad can a whole summer spent crying in my room really be? Surely no worse than crying in the men's toilets?! *This is it,* I think as I mop up my own tears from the men's bathroom floor. *I have reached an all-time low.*

"Knock knock," says a familiar voice from behind me. I turn to see Joe, hovering awkwardly in the doorway.

"You can come in," I say. "It's me who's not supposed to be here."

"It's all right, I don't need to, err. . ." He sweeps his hand through his dark, curly hair. "I just wanted to say hi."

"Oh." I sniff. "Hi."

I sound so pathetic in the moment that I burst out laughing, but I'm still crying, so this weird cry-laugh sound emerges. Joe smiles too.

"M, do you want me to. . ." He sighs. "What I mean is, it's obvious you've been crying. But if you want I can pretend it's not obvious and we can both just go about our days, because I know sometimes when you're crying you don't want anyone to draw attention to it. Or, if you want, I *can* see you crying and we can both acknowledge it and hug. Or I could go and get Aimee and she can hug you because she's much less awkward than me and it will probably be more fulfilling. I realize, now, that if you want me not to

39

notice, I've probably already ruined it by pointing out that I noticed."

Joe rambles a lot, especially when he feels uncomfortable.

"You give very fulfilling hugs, Joe," I say. "I'll take one please."

He nods and dutifully moves towards me. We have a solemn hug by the urinals.

"It'll be OK, M," he says, coming out of the hug. "Look, I get a whistle." He grins and points at the whistle around his neck. That's something I've always admired about Joe. He takes so much joy in the little things.

"Very snazzy," I say.

He goes to leave, blowing his whistle at me. "On the double, Burton," he barks. "I want these toilets spick and span by the time I get back." He marches out of the room. I look out the window and see him striding all the way down the side of the pool towards Aimee. They both climb up on their tall lifeguard chairs and start laughing about something. It's still early, but the sun is already shining brightly and its rays sparkle across the pool.

People have begun arriving and started to claim their spots with towels on sunloungers. The most popular spots are obviously on the little fake beach. One or two people are struggling to put up their massive, blue-and-white striped umbrellas. Some are already in the water or sipping on refreshing drinks from brightly coloured glasses. I can see Belinda swanning around with a drink herself, pretending not to see people waving at her to take their order. Everyone looks shiny (in a good way) and relaxed. The heat is still rising and it feels like there's a sense of anticipation in the air for the summer that's to come.

It looks *glorious* out there.

And I'm stuck in the toilets. With a mop.

I feel like an imposter. Like I'm an observer at a strange human zoo, peering in at a summer I was never supposed to be a part of. *Don'tcrydon'tcrydon'tcry*. This was a bad plan, that's all. But I can make a new one. I'm just going to finish my shift and hand my notice in at the end of the day. That's all I need to focus on.

I move round a corner, behind the cubicles, and start cleaning. After a minute or two the repetitive swipes across the floor are almost soothing ... if I imagine it's not really happening. I never got dumped. I'm not actually here. I'm actually in Spain right now. I hear the odd laugh from outside and pretend it's me and Freddie. I hear the occasional splash and pretend we're splashing in his parents' pool...

I get so distracted that I don't hear someone come in

behind me, until I hear the unmistakable unzipping of a pair of trousers.

I freeze.

Oh my DAYS. Nooo. *No no no no.* There was supposed to be a sign on the door! CLEANING IN PROGRESS. In big red letters! How did they miss it?! And what do I do now?!?! What if I see something that scars me for life? And then get arrested for sexual harassment, like I *actively attempted* to see it?! That would be just my luck!

Quickly, before I can really think about it, and I'm *absolutely not sure why*, I leap out from behind the cubicle, pointing the mop at the unsuspecting bathroom goer.

"STOP!" I call, mop outstretched in one hand like a sword. I cover my eyes with my other hand. "WOMAN ALERT! WOMAN ALERT!"

I hear them stumbling backwards.

"Oh my goodness," a deep, male voice says breathlessly. "I am so, *so* sorry. I didn't see you there."

"There's a sign," I squeak, eyes still covered.

"Oh my goodness," he says again. "I'm so sorry. I must have missed it. I swear, I don't know where my head's at today. I've had a stressful morning. I must have walked right past it."

"Are you decent?" I say, my voice still coming out like a mouse.

"Oh, yes, yes," he says.

I slowly lift my hand away from my eyes.

And reveal ... possibly *the prettiest boy* I have ever seen in my entire life.

And I read girls' magazines. That is sixteen years' worth of *very pretty boys*.

Big, almond-shaped brown eyes framed in long, dark lashes blink at me. "I'm Jake," he says with a wave. "I'm sorry, I didn't quite catch your name."

"I'm..." I start, but then get lost somewhere in his face. Maybe the nose. It's a very pretty nose. And noses aren't usually pretty. They're quite an odd feature, really. *Who am I?*

"...Maya," I finally remember.

"It's lovely to meet you, Maya." He smiles. "Um, I'm not usually so forward with girls I barely know, but given we're probably past formalities... Are you OK?"

For a moment I try to work out what he means and then... *Oh my days*. I was so distracted by his entrance that I stopped crying, but I realize I probably have a red, tear-streaked face and giant, puffy eyes. How embarrassing. My instinct is to brush it off, but there's something about Jake's gentle manner and kind, open face that makes me feel like he won't judge me. We hold eye contact for a moment too long.

"I'm sorry," he says. "Don't answer that. We don't know each other. It was rude of me." He bites his lip for a second, as if thinking. "I know! Would you like to see a picture of a puppy instead? Puppies always cheer me up."

"Um," I say. My instinct is to say "it's fine" and back away. I don't usually get into long conversations with *strange boys*. But then I don't usually hang around crying in boys' bathrooms. And who wouldn't want to see a picture of a puppy? "Always."

He leans towards me and gets out his phone. As he comes closer, an amazing boy-cologne smell washes over me and I inhale deeply. Then I realize this is an *incredibly weird* thing to do, especially as I was already lurking in the boys' bathrooms. I reach for a tissue, trying to pass off my sniffing as a result of crying, rather than creeping. He opens up his photos and shows me a picture of the cutest golden labrador puppy bounding around a garden.

"My aunt got him last week," Jake says.

"Ohhh," I say. "He's *adorable*."

"Yep, but he's *trouble*," says Jake. "That's actually why I'm here. My aunt's finding it too much with work and the new puppy, so *obviously* I volunteered to dog-sit."

"Obviously," I agree, thinking that sounds like a much better summer job than mine.

"I want to be a vet, so it's good practice, I guess." He laughs.

I frown. Why does this sound so familiar? Have I met him before? I'm *sure* I haven't.

"Anyway, if you ever need some dog therapy, my aunt's just down the road from here." He puts his phone away and stretches his hand out towards me. "I'd better go for my swim now. It was great to meet you, Maya."

I put my hand out to shake his, when I notice a spot of blood on his white T-shirt.

"Oh!" I point at his upper arm. "Are you OK? You're bleeding!"

"Oh, goodness!" He looks down. "That must be from this morning. I'm fine, thanks, I've got some plasters."

He fumbles in his backpack and pulls out a box. "Actually, would you mind? Sorry..." He gestures to his arm. "It's hard to do one-handed."

I smile. "Sure."

As I unwrap the plaster, he pulls back his T-shirt and wipes the blood from his arm. I get another whiff of cologne and try to avoid smelling him again as I lean in.

"What happened?" I ask as I lay the plaster on his warm, bare skin.

"Oh, just a few scratches," he answers. "This poor little kitten was stuck up a tree."

I jolt upwards. This sounds even *more* familiar... *Do I know this boy, somehow? Surely not?* He's so beautiful, I feel like I'd definitely remember him. Before I can try to place him, my head crashes into his from moving so quickly. Our skulls clash together with a painful bump.

"Oh no, I'm so sorry!" I exclaim. "I tried helping with one injury and gave you another!"

He laughs, clutching his forehead. "It's fine, it's fine. Can't feel a thing." Well, that's a lie, because my own head is throbbing. But he's being very sporting about it. Freddie just used to laugh at my clumsiness, like when I dropped our Bunsen burners on the floor in science... Which wasn't especially helpful, particularly when I was doing most of the work. (Still, I suppose it *was* funny).

Jake smooths the plaster down with his thumb. "Anyway, thank you so much, Maya. I'll see you around."

He turns back at the doorway and beams at me. I return the smile weakly. After he's gone I realize I've been distracted from thinking about Freddie for a full ten minutes ... and then my phone buzzes.

It's Freddie.

Finally, *is this it?!?!* Has he come to his senses? I can't look at the message. What if he still wants me come to

Spain?! Would I go now? Could we go back and pretend the last few days never happened? Even though he totally pied me off via text and invited another girl on holiday in my place? Maybe – maybe – he was crying so hard about our break-up that text was the only way he *could* communicate? And Lydia got the wrong end of the stick about the holiday?

I imagine taking off my rubber gloves and flinging them in Belinda's sour face, and Freddie ordering me a taxi that has to speed through the traffic to get to the airport. I wonder if I'm going to make it in time, but I do, obviously, and when I dash through arrivals I leap into his arms and he holds me tightly and we have a passionate kiss and *everyone is watching. . .*

I finally look at the message.

It wasn't about the hat. I just don't know where my head's at. Sorry you have to spend the summer cleaning (Lydia told me). That sucks.
x

Sorry you have to spend the summer cleaning?!?!?
That sucks?!?!?
Is that *seriously* all he has to say to me?

"Lydia told me." Yes, because they're together right now, probably in a car on the way to the airport where

I'm supposed to be. Me. Not Lydia.

My heart, which was beating a million mph at the sight of his message, slows way back down. With a heavy heart I pick up my mop again. Yes, Freddie, it really "sucks".

CHAPTER

FOUR

After three painful hours of scrubbing the floor, and wondering what Freddie and Lydia are up to (have they landed yet? What snacks did they buy on the plane? Did their hands brush as they both reached into a bag of nuts?) I head outside for my lunch break. The sun is beating down intensely by now and the pool has started to fill up. People are *splashing around in the water* and *reclining on sunloungers*. I severely dislike each and every single one of them.

"Heyyy!!" shouts Aimee from across the other side of the pool. She's sporting giant sunglasses and a Hawaiian-style flower necklace.

"I hate you!" I call back in response.

"Love you too!" she replies.

When I finally reach her and Joe, she holds out her drink to me from aloft in her chair. It's in a coconut. "Virgin colaaahda smoothie?"

I push it away sulkily, then regret it. It looks really good.

"Suit yourself." Aimee ruffles her flowers. "It was made for me specially, courtesy of Hot Sauce."

"Hot Sauce?" I ask.

"The hot waiter," Joe stage whispers behind one hand.

"But we can't call him that, obvs," Aimee adds. "He made it for me on the house and pushed it across the counter with a *very intense stare*. Earlier on he gave me extra chocolate sauce on my ice cream, hence the name."

I turn to look behind me.

"No!" Aimee hisses and grabs my arm. "Don't look! He'll know we're talking about him! God, Maya, you're so unsubtle."

"Less subtle than *Hot Sauce?*" I raise one eyebrow.

"Hey, I came up with that!" Joe cries.

"It's hardly the enigma code," I say.

"Check him out on your walk back to the toilets." Aimee winks. "You won't regret it. If you can get a proper look. He's spent half the day writing something down on till roll. I bet it's *poetry*."

"Fascinating. Anyway, I came to tell you something," I start. "I just had a really weird experience in the toilets."

"Oh my God," says Aimee. "I know we're close, M, but this might be TMI."

"What? Ew, no! I mean an experience with a boy."

Joe and Aimee's eyebrows fly off their foreheads. "Maya!" Aimee calls. "You dark horse!"

"NO," I say. "Not like that!!!" But Joe and Aimee are already in fits of laughter. "Oh, forget it," I say. "I'm going to make *new friends.* Maybe with Hot Sauce."

I turn around and start walking back to the cleaning supply cupboard. I can still hear Joe and Aimee cackling behind me like witches. I glance over towards the café area. It's a little pop-up tiki café surrounded by stools, set at the back of the pool under a straw roof on stilts. There's a sign that says, "Tiki Your Time, Takie A Drink. . ."

Behind the counter is cast in shadow, and I can just make out a mysterious, slim figure skulking in the darkness. *Come on*, I think. *Step into the light so I can spy on you please*. I squint and peer a little closer. Which turns out to be *the most stupid thing to do ever* because I am, obviously, walking right beside a large body of water.

It must happen incredibly quickly, but the next three to five seconds feel like they take place in slow motion. I lose my footing. I stumble. I briefly make eye contact with a small child by the side of the pool, who opens his mouth in sympathetic horror. I look towards the water in sheer panic. I stick my arms out and move them in little circles like a windmill. For a moment I think I might just have saved it. I think, *maybe I'm not going to fall in after all. Maybe I'll just carry on walking and everyone will laugh a bit at my weird windmill arms but ultimately get on with their day.*

But then I, obviously, fall in.

I hit the water with a giant SPLASH. My mouth and nose fill with water. *Gaurghhhhhhh!!!!! Well,* I think as I sink underwater, *I might as well not have bothered doing windmill arms at all. That way I'd still have fallen in, but at least I'd have fallen in like a normal person!* Then I wonder... Shall I just *stay* underwater? Surely it would be less humiliating to drown than it would to get out at this point?! Everyone has sympathy for a young girl who meets an untimely, watery death. *No one* has sympathy for an idiot who slips into a pool trying to get a good look at a "hot waiter".

I keep sinking for a millisecond, genuinely contemplating the possibility of death. It takes approximately sixty seconds for a grown adult to drown. It's only been about five seconds so far, so that's a whole lot more oxygen deprivation to commit to. But then the decision is made for me, and a giant, muscular pair of arms reaches in and wrenches me upwards.

I break the surface of the water, coughing and spluttering. I sense a warm, solid body behind me, steadily guiding me towards the edge of the pool. Even though I am wheezing and spraying up water from my nose, and should really be concentrating on getting oxygen into my lungs, I can't help but glance at the arms wrapped around me. They're so ... *big*.

Did I die? Is this heaven?

Then I see Joe's concerned face bobbing in the water. He must have dived in after me, too. That would make sense given that he and Aimee are the lifeguards on duty. So who is this mysterious, big-armed rescuer?!

"You're all right," says an Australian accent in my ear. "Gotcha."

"Thank you," I rasp, gasping for breath.

When we reach the edge of the pool the giant pair of arms heaves me up over the side. Then they reach up beside me and I finally get a look at the arms' owner.

Oh my days.

He's H-U-G-E.

A toned, tanned body emerges from the water ... and keeps emerging. He's *tall*. Blond hair glints in the sun as he climbs on to the decking. He leans in towards

53

me, his head on one side. Water slides off his built arms and down his six-pack. *Six-pack*. Who has a six-pack?! In real life, not on TV?! I try not to stare at it. Them. But it's hard. They're so big and defined it's like they're their own separate beings.

"Are you all right?" There's that Australian accent again.

I nod. Thankfully he seems to put my lack of speech down to having nearly drowned, not being distracted by his stomach.

"Are you OK, Maya?" Joe has clambered out of the pool and rushed to my side. He crouches beside Ripped Boy, who pats him on the shoulder so vigorously that Joe's entire body shakes.

"She'll be fine, mate," says the Australian.

Suddenly Aimee looms over me, standing behind the boys and blocking out the sun. "Jeez, sorry I laughed at your weird toilet experience, M," she says. "There was no need to go and drown yourself!"

Australian's eyes shift to one side. "Uhhhh," he says.

I am going to *kill* Aimee.

She keeps going, putting a hand on his right shoulder. "Oh, thank God you were here..." She gestures for him to say his name.

"Adam," says Australian.

"*Adam!* I was on a break, so Lord knows what would have happened if you weren't around."

I feel like Aimee's on a constant "break".

"Well, actually, I was..." says Joe. But Aimee interrupts again.

"She's always been a bit unsteady on her feet, this one." She nods her head at me. "I'll never understand how someone so organized cannot maintain basic coordination of her limbs. We'll have to keep a closer eye on her in future. Won't we, Maya?"

Adam looks at me, then, and winks. "No worries. I'll keep an eye out too, *Maya*," he says. Then he gets up. I stand, too, partly just to prove I am actually capable of doing it without falling over. Adam takes one arm and Joe holds the other.

"I'm fine, I'm fine," I assert.

"I'd better go, I'm going to be late for my lesson," says Adam. He gestures behind him and suddenly I notice a group of children standing beside us. "It's not quite like riding the waves over in Costa Rica, but someone's gotta teach these kids how to swim, ey?"

For the second time today I have an incredibly strong sense of déjà vu. Did I bash my skull on the bottom of the pool? Has the sun gone to my head after only one day working at Casa Nadar?! But I've barely been outside.

Maybe the chemical fumes from the cleaning products? I'm *so sure* I've heard this somewhere. . .

Adam heads over to the kids calling, "All right! Phones down now! Time to get in!" (I see the little boy who looked "concerned" for me as I fell in the pool, laughing over a picture of me, mid-windmill arms. Remind me never to have children.) Adam winks at me again and takes the kids down to the shallow end of the pool. Joe heads back to his lifeguard chair, muttering under his breath about Aimee and "at least one of them paying some attention".

After they're gone Aimee whistles. "Nice work, M," she says. "Falling in the pool. Very *damsel in distress*."

"I wasn't. . ."

"There were serious *vibes* between you." She moves her eyebrows up and down.

"No." I shake my head.

She raises her eyebrows higher.

"I *just broke up* with Freddie."

She raises her eyebrows so high they basically lift off her forehead.

"I mean, he has a nice . . . ahem. . ."

"Physique?" Aimee suggests.

"Well. . ." I can feel myself blushing.

"*I knew it!* I knew you weren't blind!" she screams. And we both start laughing.

Once we've finished giggling about Adam's well-developed abdominal muscles, Aimee walks me to the towel rack to "wrap me up nice and warm" and get me a new, dry uniform. (On the way over she dubs Adam as "Hot Plate", because "his stomach is so toned you could literally eat off it".)

"Gotta get back to the grind now, chica," she says, after speculating for ten more minutes about Hot Plate's protein intake, and her already-forming tan lines. "Are you gonna be OK?"

"I'm fine, I'm fine. Honestly." I wave her off. "Unless Belinda takes a close look at the mortar between the floor tiles. Then she'll realize I didn't finish scrubbing and Adam will have saved my life for nothing, because she will *actually murder me.*"

Aimee laughs. "I PLEADED with her to make you a lifeguard again earlier, by the way. For the FIVE HUNDREDTH time. I offered her everything: my sports skills, my sparkly eyeshadow, my sweat and blood. But to no avail, I'm afraid."

"Thanks for trying." I smile. The fact I have such a good friend makes me feel slightly better about cleaning loos.

Aimee heads back to "help" Joe. I sit quietly for a moment on a bench by the lockers. Today has been ...

odd. This morning feels like a very long time ago and my planned dreamy break with Freddie seems an eternity away. I look at the time on my phone. I should be heading through the Spanish countryside to Freddie's family holiday home right now.

"Something on your mind?" says a voice from behind me.

I nearly jump out of my skin. I turn sharply to see a boy a few metres away, leaning against the lockers. Half his face is hidden under a long, dark fringe, but I can see some chiselled cheekbones poking out.

"Er..." I answer.

"Sorry, I'm being nosy," he says, springing away from the lockers and coming a little closer. He brushes his hair away from his face. "It's just that you have that look I sometimes get when I'm right in the middle of writing a song."

"You write songs?" I ask.

"Yup." He pats his pocket and pulls out a long scrap of till roll. "Been scribbling lyrics today, actually."

Ah. So *this* must be the mysterious Hot Sauce.

"Can I hear some?" I ask.

"Uhhh." He flushes and stares down at his shoes.

"Sorry," I say. "Now *I'm* being nosy."

He looks up at me and smiles. Wow, Aimee was right. He does have a *very* intense stare. In a good way.

"Well, I started it." He pauses. "I know I'm a complete stranger but, if you do ever want to talk. . ."

That stare again. Kind of like he sees all of me – and all my problems – and really *gets* them on a deeper level. Even though that can't possibly be true, because we just met and he knows nothing about me.

"Is this your first day?" I ask.

"Yup," he says. "Working the day shifts here and I've got a few other jobs in the evenings. More café work, the local supermarket, babysitting. . ." Wow. Suddenly I feel ashamed at feeling so hard done by about a few cleaning shifts. "Trying to save enough to go on a tour with the band," he continues. "Anyway, I need to head back, my break's over, but it was good to meet you. I'm Noah, by the way."

"I'm Maya," I say.

I watch him walk back to the café, where a group of girls have already crowded round waiting for him to serve them. I watch him solemnly retrieve an apple from a cupboard and lay it out like he's about to perform an operation on it, when he looks back at me and catches me staring. The corner of his mouth curls in a smile. I blush and get back to work.

At the end of the day I change out of my uniform with Aimee and we head to meet Joe at the gate. My fingers are red raw from cleaning products and if Aimee says one more time about how tiring her day of *sitting* has been, I might bash her with my mop.

"I can't BELIEVE how cold Belinda is being about this lifeguarding issue!" Aimee says again. "I thought for sure she'd cackle over you with a mop for a day and then relent. I gave her my best puppy dog eyes and NOTHING."

Aimee is clearly distraught about her puppy dog eyes being rendered so ineffective. I laugh. "It's fine, Ames, honestly, cleaning isn't *so* bad."

I don't sound very convincing. I catch her up on my weirdly intense conversation with Hot Sauce instead, and finally tell her about the toilet interaction with the dog-sitter boy this morning (who Aimee predictably dubs "Hot Dog").

Then Aimee says, "Flirting with *three hot guys* in one day, M. Did you fill out a form or something?"

I stop walking. My eyes widen. I halt so abruptly that Aimee nearly goes crashing into my back and we almost end up in the pool again.

"What?!" cries Aimee.

"I think... I think I..." I rub my temples. "Ames, this is going to sound properly mental, but..." Suddenly I remember. I know where I know all those guys from, why I've been having an overwhelming feeling of déjà vu all day, why I've felt so odd and dream-like. I think I *do* know these boys. Or at least ... what sounds spookily like them on paper. Each and every one of them sounds *exactly like a boy from my magazine!!!*

"Ames..." I say again, but she's already dragging me towards the door.

"Come on," she orders. "Joe's waiting."

I'm too speechless to try and explain myself. We exit Casa Nadar and head towards where Joe's standing on the corner, waiting for us and playing on his phone. But someone else is waiting, too.

Three someones.

Joe sees my open-mouthed stare and follows my gaze behind him. Aimee claps her hands together gleefully and starts bouncing on her toes. There they all are. Standing beside one another. Hot Sauce, Hot Plate and Hot Dog. As we come out, they all look up at the same time and wave at me.

"NO WAY!!" Aimee laughs and *actually rubs her hands together.* "I think they're all waiting for you, M!!"

Oh. My. Days.

CHAPTER

FIVE

After the world's most awkward walk home, I sit on my bed, staring into space. This is *not* how I pictured my summer. *At all.* And it's just getting weirder and weirder by the minute. What on earth *was* today?!

When we stepped out of Casa Nadar, Jake, Adam and Noah all started walking towards me at once. I tried to slink off into the shadows but Aimee grabbed my arm and waved at them, yelling, "HAAAAIIIII!"

Jake flashed me that warm, open smile I remembered from this morning. Adam rolled up his sleeves, purposefully or accidentally baring his muscles, and waved. Noah swept a hand through his fringe and served a quick nod with a side of intense stare.

Maybe I should have been thinking about the *three*

stunning boys waiting for me after work (according to Aimee anyway – I'm still not convinced!). But all I could think about was what a freakish coincidence this was, that literally last night I filled out a romance quiz and now here were three near-identical guys to the ones I . . . erm . . . ordered. Was someone playing a practical joke on me?! I wouldn't put it past Aimee and her sick sense of humour. I glared at her.

"What?" she mouthed back at me.

"Uhhh," Joe said as he came up behind the three boys. "I think I'll go." He pointed in the direction of his house. I could barely see him peeking out from behind Adam's giant shoulders.

"Yeah, cool, Joe, see ya tomorrow," Aimee waved distractedly, not making eye contact. She was looking at the three boys like a dog that had spied three roast chickens.

I craned my neck around Adam and waved at Joe. He gave me a small smile and went on his way.

"G'd evening ladies." Adam spoke first. I stopped glaring at Aimee and turned to face the boys. "Maya, I'm glad to see you made it out alive." Adam winked.

"Uh, yeah, heart still beating, blood still circulating, glands still secreting. . ." I tailed off.

"That's her way of saying yes, thanks," Aimee

interrupted. "She likes *biology*," she added behind the back of her hand.

There was an awkward silence. All three guys were looking between each other, almost sizing each other up. Adam was frowning at Noah's haircut, Noah was staring at Jake's cool shoes, probably wondering where he could buy a pair, and Jake's eyes were widened at Adam's arms. They all looked confused, like they were trying to figure something out, *perhaps* realizing they'd all come to wait for the same person. If Aimee was right, that is. *Were* they all really waiting for me?!

Then a little bark interrupted us. We all noticed the small, golden furry creature standing behind Jake's feet.

"This is Stefan," he said, reaching down to pick up the puppy. "I was walking him and just happened to pass this way."

"Yeah, and I was, just, er." Noah ran his hands through his hair and gazed at the sky. "Inspired to write a song about that tree."

Aimee snorted. "Sure. All three of you are just coincidentally here at the same time as Maya's shift finishes. Cool, cool, cool. Shall we all just coincidentally walk back in the same direction towards her house?"

Jake became increasingly interested in the puppy.

Noah became even more hidden under his fringe. Adam laughed and offered Aimee his arm.

"A woman after my own heart. Shall we?"

Aimee took his arm and then reached for Noah's. "Come on, Hot Sau— Er, I mean, Noah." She grabbed him and sandwiched herself between him and Adam, and began marching forwards. Stefan bounded after them, barking, and Jake laughed, saying, "Well, I guess Stefan has spoken." We followed behind the others.

And that is how Aimee kidnapped three unsuspecting victims and brought them back to my house. Thankfully, she walked with us so I barely had to make any conversation. At one point I explained what *actually happens* when you get a suntan (all tanning is actually skin damage; the melanocytes in your skin are triggered by the sun to produce melanin, to protect it from further damage) but Aimee cut me off pretty abruptly. *Right* in the middle of the word "melanocyte". She gave me a warning stare as if to say "make better small talk". Personally I would much rather learn about melanocytes than what someone's having for dinner, but maybe that's just me.

When we got home I glimpsed Dad's face peeking out from the window. Even from a great distance I could see his eyes bugging out of his head at the sight of the approaching troop of boys.

I went into the house and we all said our goodbyes, and when I got to my room I could still hear Aimee laughing all the way down the street. That girl is pure evil.

I get a message from her.

Thanks to me they all know where you live now, so I expect 20% commission of the flowers/chocolates you will receive.

Actually . . . Make that 50%.

Screw it, just hand over the lot.

I stew for five minutes, trying to ignore her as a sign of how greatly annoyed I am with her for pushing me on these poor, unsuspecting boys who were just walking their dogs and communing with their tree-muses. It's *mortifying.* Freddie, who I dated for three whole months, seems to have forgotten about me in five minutes. What makes Aimee think that three unattainably gorgeous boys would be this interested in me?!

You're mad. I reply. **They were obviously all just minding their own business and you kidnapped them.**

Sure. Cool, cool, she replies.

I'm about to argue again when, at that very moment, my phone buzzes three different times with three unknown numbers. I blink. Huh? This is *highly unusual*. The only people to ever contact me are Dad, Aimee and Joe. What is going on today? Who is it???

But, before I open the messages, I have a strange gut feeling I already know the answer. And a strong sense of who to blame.

> Hi Maya. Hope you don't mind me messaging but Aimee gave me your number. Stefan was wondering if you wanted to help take him for a walk this weekend? He's sick of just me for company! ;) Jake :)

> Hey M. Aimee passed me your number. Do you fancy heading down to the assault course on Sat? Adam

> Hi Maya. I hope you're feeling a little less lost than you seemed earlier on today. I have a spare ticket to a Summer of Cyanide gig this weekend. Aimee said you were into them and would probs want to come? So sweet to meet a fellow SoC fan! Noah x

OH MY DAYS. THIS IS NOT HAPPENING.

Who even are *Summer of Cyanide?!* They sound *terrifying!*

I am shocked. Utterly, utterly flabbergasted. I've never been more taken aback in my life. Is this for real?! Has Aimee *paid them* to ask me out?!?! And it's so . . . *sudden.* We only met today. How could we know whether we wanted to go out with each other yet? Surely that sort of decision requires months of considered thought and data collection?

This goes against *every instinct* in my calm, collected, ordered brain. I'm only just out of a relationship with *one* guy. I mean, yes, all right, I did fill out that quiz. But only to prove to myself that I might one day conceptualize *the idea of being with someone else.*

I wasn't expecting them to all *turn up on my doorstep the following day!!!*

I should be eating ice cream . . . and Jaffa cakes . . . and . . . and wallowing and spending time with my friends and letting time heal my wounds, etc. etc., and *then* when I am finally done crying and stewing and obsessing and making everyone sick of me, *THEN* I would pick myself up and *carefully select* my chosen partner for my next relationship. Emphasis on *careful.* To make sure *I NEVER GET HURT AGAIN.*

But then, I thought I was careful about Freddie and look where that got me.

There's a soft knock on my door. Dad's glasses peep round the frame.

"Can I come in?" he asks.

"Sure," I say.

"So ... made some new friends?" he asks, edging into the room. He's trying to play it cool but his eyebrows literally couldn't get any higher and his smile is like a letterbox.

"*Aimee* made me some new friends," I reply.

"Haven't unpacked yet?" He changes the subject, clearly deciding not to press further. He gestures to the suitcase sticking out from under my bed. (I repacked it after Aimee threw its contents around my room #nojudgement).

"Uh, no," I admit.

"About your holiday..." he says. "You can talk to your old dad, you know."

"I know." I nod. "I just don't like to upset you."

"I'm not upset. I'm disappointed for you, but selfishly pleased you're staying here for the entire summer." He grins.

I breathe a sigh of relief. Upsetting Dad always leaves me feeling weird and unsettled, like I've put my shoes on the wrong feet or shaved a kitten. I suspect he may just be putting on a brave face for me, but I'll take it.

We smile at each other awkwardly for a moment. Then Dad moves forward and pats me on the shoulder. He points at the suitcase. "Shall we?" he asks.

I nod. We spend the next fifteen minutes *conscientiously* unfolding my clothes and putting them back in their proper places (I have to redo most of what Dad does – he's as chaotic as Aimee – but it's nice doing it together anyway). When we're done Dad takes the suitcase back up to the loft. Surprisingly, getting rid of it does actually feel like a load off my shoulders.

After he's gone I glance back at my phone, which I've been trying to ignore. It all just feels so overwhelming. I wasn't expecting to get dumped by Freddie, and having been dumped by Freddie I *definitely* wasn't expecting to get asked out by three new swoon-worthy guys. I don't know... Am I ready to think about going out with someone else yet? The idea of going on one of these dates seems *completely terrifying*.

I pick it up and glance through all their messages again. Dog-walking with an incredibly sensitive, smart aspiring vet. Assault-coursing (I have to google it – can't believe people do this for fun) with a ripped, charming backpacker... Gigging with a mysterious, ambitious, edgy musician... I feel numb and utterly dumbfounded about this whole situation, but I can't pretend these don't all sound like *the dream*, on paper.

I sigh and pick up my phone.

"Ames, tell me the truth: did you force all these boys to ask me out?" Aimee's face appears on my screen. She's lying on her bed with her phone above her, chewing something.

"UGH!" she yells, sitting up. "I'm SO upset that Freddie has destroyed your confidence in this way, M. NO. I mean, all right, I told Noah you were a SoC fan when he mentioned he had tickets at the weekend, which was a teeny, tiny white lie. But get a clue. They all want to go out with you."

I bite my lip. "Do you think I should?"

"Oh my God, Maya. Get out there. Play the field. Sow your oats. You're wasted on obsessing over Freddie and I genuinely think this would be good for you."

Aimee hardly ever says anything serious, so she must really mean this. I take a deep breath. "All right, Aimee... I'll do it."

"YAY!!!!!!" She does a celebratory dance. As soon as I say the words it all feels real and my heart starts hammering. No going back now.

"All right," I say hesitantly. "So which one?"

"*Excusez-moi?*" She blows a giant pink bubble, which pops in her face.

"Which one should I choose?"

"*Excusez-MOI?*" she repeats, mid-chew.

"Which one?"

"I'm sorry, I am confused by your use of the terms 'choose' and 'which'."

"I'm confused by your confusion."

"GO OUT WITH THEM ALL, YOU DOPE!" she yells, sitting up.

I inhale sharply. "Aimee, I can't *go out with them all*," I say.

"Why not?"

"Because there's *three of them*."

"Yes."

"And there's *one of me*."

"Yes."

"So ... it doesn't add up!!!"

"My maths isn't that bad, M." Aimee rolls her eyes.

"Have you never watched any reality dating show ever?" I continue. "Since when does seeing more than one person *ever go well?!*"

Aimee puts her hand out, as if to say "chill out". "M, no one's asking you to become a bigamist. Or even a serial snogger. Just *get to know them!*"

"*Get to know them*," I repeat softly.

"Yeah," Aimee says. She leans her face really close to her camera. "What people usually do before they pledge their undying love."

She's *quite unsubtly* referring to how I singled Freddie out before I had actually spoken a word to him. Still, maybe she has a point.

"*Get to know them*," I repeat again.

"Got to go, M, dinner's ready." She hangs up and I sit on the bed computing all this *very new and confusing* information. Am I *really* contemplating going out with three different guys?!

I lie back on my bed and flick on to social media, thinking I'll forget about this for a while and reply to each of them tomorrow. Or is that rude? Should I be more thoughtful about the length of time I take over this? Can I reply to them all at once or is that like a betrayal? Should I space out my replies to make it less snakey?

See? I'm terrible at this dating-three-people thing already! I can't even *text* three people!!!

Suddenly, Freddie's face pops up on my screen next to Lydia's. (So they didn't lose their suitcases in a terrible airport admin mix-up or get stuck in huge, mind-numbing delays or have their flights cancelled altogether due to awful weather conditions, then?) I take a look at Freddie's Instagram. There's a picture of him and Lydia sharing a huge platter of paella. In classic Freddie fashion, he's making one of the prawns walk across the table. And he's smiling. *Smiling.* It doesn't *look* like the fake, I'm-heartbroken-but-soldiering-on kind of smile either. It looks like ... well, a normal smile.

Something inside me snaps. I turn my screen off, so I don't have to look at their happy, mid-holiday faces.

Then turn it back on.

> **Hi Jake. I would love to take Stefan for a walk! Can't promise I'll be better company for him than you but I'll give it a shot... M x**

> **Hi Adam. I'll tell you now I had to google what an assault course was but I'm up for giving it a go, if you're willing to teach a rookie! M x**

> **Hi Noah. Oh, yes please – it would be great to come see SoC! Have never seen them live before x**

(Or heard any of their music before, but oh well.)

I put my phone away for good and stare at my ceiling, breathing in, and out. When school ended I thought I had everything under control. Everything was decided. I was supposed to spend the summer with Freddie and his family, having fun in-between reading and prepping for next year, messaging Joe and Aimee mindless updates. Now, apparently I'm not dating Freddie but *three different guys* and going on "assault courses" and to see scary bands I've never heard of. Surely, this is all happening to someone else, not me... This *cannot be my life.*

I do not like it when plans go awry.

I keep breathing in, and out, in, and out... Then I spot the corner of the "dream summer romance" quiz poking out from under my pillow, from when I fell asleep doing it the other day. I pull it out and stare at it. Despite dabbling in my magazine's astrological predictions I've never *completely believed* in destiny or fate before (I am a scientist, after all), but it really is weirdly similar... I get a little chill down my spine.

My own plan's gone totally wrong, so maybe it's time to trust in the universe's.

CHAPTER

 **six**

The next day at Casa Nadar, it's nearly the end of my shift and I'm *freaking out*. This evening is my first of *three* dates. All my "trust in the universe" Zen rubbish from last night has completely evaporated. What kind of strange brain spasm prompted me to agree to go out with *three guys?!*

I spent all day worrying and running back and forth between the toilets and Aimee for pep talks. The sixth time Belinda caught me outside, she puffed out her chest even more, went properly red and shouted, "For the last time, Burton, you are here to disinfect tiles, not sit outside *yakking with your friends.*" Oh, how I wish I was a lifeguard. If I was sitting outside with Aimee and Joe today, I would still have been nervous, but at least I would have been nervous sipping a smoothie in the sun rather than panicking in a dingy bathroom all alone.

"It's fine, M," Aimee soothes, sipping her orange and pink "sunrise smoothie" with a green umbrella. (I'm outside, yet again, but Belinda's patrolling the indoor pool so she shouldn't catch me). "Just go out with each of them once, then you can decide who to crack on with." She slurps through her straw.

"Well, it might not be a problem, anyway," I say. "Because I might *die* on this assault course."

"Nah, Hot Plate will be there to catch you in his *giant arms* if you fall," Joe jokes. We all look over at Adam, showing a group of nine-year-olds the correct diving motion by the side of the pool. "God, they really are *big*," Joe exclaims. He glances down at his own arms with a sigh.

"What if he's not standing behind me?!" I panic, looking again at the picture of the *towering climbing wall* at the course.

"Look, if you're really worried, I can coach you on some stuff. I know that assault course," Joe says.

"Really?" Aimee looks pointedly at Joe's arms.

"Ha *ha*, Ames," Joe replies sarcastically. "Yes, I do. I used to go there with my cousins. It's really not that bad. Kids go there!"

I look at my phone again, at the picture of the giant wall. "Do they ever return?" I ask.

"All right, come on." Joe looks at his watch. "We've got an hour until Adam finishes. Shall we practise some stuff? I can bring the hula hoops out back. And we can use a bench as a balance beam."

"I guess I've got nothing to lose." I shrug.

"This I *have* to see." Aimee jumps down from her lifeguard chair. "I can't believe you go to the assault course, Joe! Are you a secret *gym-goer* too?"

Joe ignores that comment. "Um, Aimee, you're not done for another hour," he says.

"It's OK. No one's died swimming in our town in the history of time. How likely is it, really, that someone will drown in the next hour?"

Joe simply raises an eyebrow at her and points to the chair in reply.

"*Drat*," she curses. "Please take photos."

Joe and I head to the locker room. "OK, balance beams," he says. "At the assault course these are much higher up than this and if you fall off, you land in the mud."

"Joy," I say. Again, *why did I agree to this?!* I sigh. I'm supposed to be relaxing with a book on a beautiful Spanish hilltop right now!

"Up, Burton," he barks. He gets his phone out to time me. "You have to make it to the end of the bench and back in ten seconds, without falling. Ready?"

I jump up on the bench and nod. Joe seems like a different person when he's in "training mode". He's usually rambly and uncertain. Now he seems very sure of himself. I try to imagine him at the assault course with his cousins. I've never seen this side of him before.

"Set... GO!"

I take one step along the bench...

...And instantly fall off.

Joe hoots. I glare at him from my position on the floor.

"Sorry, sorry." He coughs, as if he might pass off his *manic laughter* as a cold. He hands me his arm and pulls me up. I dust myself down.

"Ready?" he says again.

We go a second time. And a third time. And a fourth time. Every single time I fall off, but I at least start making it further towards the end of the bench before I do. Joe is commentating on my progress.

"Burton makes it a third step ... and a fourth... Will she make it to the end?! She turns, she ... oh, *oh!* She wobbles! But she expertly regains balance and turns. Will this be her... Oh, no, she falls again."

By the end of it I am in fits of laughter, and we decide

we've done enough of the balance beam. Joe brings out some neon hula hoops from the supply cupboard and lays them on the floor.

"These are for the mid-summer luau party," he explains. "We're going to use them as tyres." He holds one up in the air, by his shin. "This is what height they'll actually be. So really lift your knees as you jump them. Ready?"

I nod. He blows his lifeguard whistle at me and I start jumping.

"Higher, Burton!" he shouts. "HIGHER."

Just as I get to the end, he lifts the last hoop and I trip over it. I go crashing forwards. "EVIL!" I shout, waving my arms around. Joe stands up quickly from his crouching position, putting his arm out to stop me toppling over. I fall straight into his left arm and he holds it around me, managing to keep me upright.

"I told you that's how high they'll be." He smirks, his face close to mine.

I extricate myself from his grip. "I'm used to Aimee bullying me, but not you, Joe."

"Never." He solemnly shakes his head.

There's a rapping on the door. We both turn towards the sound.

"Knock knock." Adam's hypnotizing Australian tones

float through the room. An arm dressed in a bright, Hawaiian shirt appears and his head follows. "There you are; I thought you'd gone walkabout. Ready, Maya?"

I'm actually *more* afraid, now that I realize I can't even balance on a bench or jump a few hula hoops, but it's too late to back out now. I nod.

"All righty, let's head." Adam grins.

I follow, turning back to flash Joe a look of panic.

"You'll be fine!" he mouths. "GO BURTON!"

Famous last words.

I stare up the huge, towering wall that apparently ten year olds pull themselves over using mere rope and core body strength. Shockingly, I managed to make it through the balance beams and tyre obstacles unscathed.

In a way the date is going well, because I am so afraid of falling to my death that I've forgotten to be anxious a) about being a serial "get-to-know-er" and b) about being on a date with a boy who has the best body I've ever laid eyes on. I glance away from the wall and across at Adam. I bet that huge, ginormous wall looks like a picket fence to him.

"Are you sure you don't want to try the balance beams again?" I ask.

Adam is on the floor doing up his shoes. "Nah, we got the beams down."

I feel a glow of pride that I actually managed to do the beams and the tyres and only fall over a few times. Practising with Joe has helped loads. But now I wish I hadn't bothered. Getting through them only means I can't avoid the wall of doom.

I can't help but think about what Freddie and Lydia are getting up to right now. Probably not contemplating climbing terrific heights with the very real possibility of plummeting at great speed to their deaths. (Did you know that fifty per cent of all falls that are three times your height are fatal? But that after falling about four-hundred-and-fifty metres you have reached terminal velocity, so your chances of death should be more or less the same? No? Well, I did know that, and unfortunately I'm the one standing in front of the *colossal great wall*). Instead of focusing too much on alternate me, safely on the ground holding Freddie's hand, I think of his smug, paella-eating grin and rally myself.

Adam finishes tying his laces on the ground and stands up. "Ready?" He holds out his hand to me.

"*Ready?*" I squeak. "Don't we need a helmet?"

"Ah, helmets are for sooks." He waves his arm.

I clear my throat. "*Ehm*, I think I might be a sook... What *is* a sook?"

He grins at me. White teeth sparkle next to his

tanned, glowing skin. I'd seen him before, obviously, but it suddenly hits me just how gorgeous this guy is. Is he *absolutely sure* he wants to go out with me?! It occurs to me that maybe he has hit his head one too many times here without suitable protection.

"A pea heart."

"Again . . . what?"

He laughs heartily. "Someone who's a bit of a wuss."

"Oh, yeah, definitely me." I nod.

He laughs from the gut. "All right, c'mon then, you big sook. Let's get you a helmet." He puts his arm around my shoulder and I swear I sink two inches into the ground.

I walk *really slowly* to get a helmet. And *really slowly* back. Then I pretend to be confused by the buckle on the helmet as if I've never seen one before. Is it possible I could spend all day here doing up my headgear? Maybe I could just watch?

Adam grins. "Come here, ya big loser." He pushes my hair back from my face and puts the helmet gently over it. Then he clips the buckle under my neck. When he's done he puts his hands on my shoulders and looks into my eyes. I look back into his. They're very blue and a sweep of blond hair falls over them.

I've forgotten my name again.

"Ready now, Maya?" He winks.

Maya. That's the one.

We approach the wall. I crane my neck back and look up to the top.

No. No. No looking up. Lookdownlookdownlookdown.

I grab the rope and heave. *OH MY DAYS.*

Am I really that heavy?!

We start climbing.

"So, Maya, you live with your dad, right?" I feel Adam's eyes on my side. Is he really trying to talk right now? It's taking *every single ounce* of breath in my body to shift myself up this wall. And we've only been going for about thirty seconds!

"Yeah," I manage, trying not to sound too breathless. "But what about *you*? Tell me about *you*." *Please please please please please don't make me talk any more!*

"What about your mum?" he carries on. "If that's not too nosy."

"She moved abroad," I wheeze. "She's a doctor in Africa."

"Oh, I'm sorry, Maya, you must miss her. That's cool though."

I do miss Mum, but we talk whenever we can, and she comes back to visit every year. I'm fine with it, but I let him think that I'm a bit emotional so he'll stop asking me questions. It works like a charm.

I'm so hot and dripping already. This has got to be *seriously unattractive.* And Adam doesn't even look like he's breaking a sweat! *Don'tdiedon'tdiedon'tdie.* I don't know whether to be more stressed about potential death or getting plum-face. Urgh, imagine if I died in the middle of having plum-face. The most humiliating way to go.

"I live with my dad for the most part too. My mum married a pom yonks ago and had a few more ankle-biters. That's partly why I'm here. My stepdad's a bit of a wombat but she likes him so, you gotta say no dramas."

I did not understand *a word of that.*

"Yeah," I agree. I pray he doesn't look at me again. Plum-face has descended. I can *only imagine* how red I am right now. "So how did you end up teaching swimming?" I ask breathlessly.

"Ran outta money." He laughs. "I try not to let material considerations get in the way, but there's only so long you can surf in Costa Rica before you've got to earn some cash. Soon as I've saved up, I'll be heading straight back for those waves."

"Will you go back to Costa Rica?" I ask.

"Nah, been there, done that." He winks. "Who knows? The world is my oyster!"

Eventually we make it to the top. I made it! *I'm alive!!!*

Adam swings one leg over and straddles the wall. He gestures his arm to the surrounding countryside and says, "Good place for a chinwag, pom."

What is a pom? I just smile. For all I know he could be calling me something incredibly insulting and I'm just smiling back at him mindlessly. I *do* understand that he's saying it's beautiful up here, though. I think.

I look out to the hills. Different shades of green stretch for miles and miles. The sun is setting and casts a golden, low-lit glow over everything. Adam looks like he's been dipped in honey. A little halo of light radiates from behind his head. Now that I've stopped worrying about my imminent death, and the shade of my cheeks, I realize how picturesque it is up here. Adam reaches forward and gently grips my left hand in his rough fingers. Something in my stomach lights up like the sky around us.

"So, Maya. Welcome to my favourite spot in Pom land. I came here as a kid when my mum first moved here."

Oh. That must have been what he was talking about earlier. He definitely said something about his mum? As I regain my breath I make a mental note to listen this time.

"What's a pom?" I finally ask.

He laughs loudly. "You," he answers. "A Brit."

"Oh, I see how it is," I say. *"Aussie."*

"Well, I'm very glad you could join me up here, pom," he says.

"Why?" I blurt. And I can hear Aimee's voice in my head, saying, "Always the charmer, M."

Adam laughs. "Um, way to put a guy on the spot. Because this way I can check you're still alive. Not drowning in any pools and that." He winks.

I resist pointing out that an assault course, without a helmet as he first suggested, is *far less safe* than being by a pool because I think he's trying to be . . . romantic?

"And, you know, you're all right." He squeezes my fingers. "You seem up for a laugh and down to earth. I like that."

I'm not sure he would say that if he could have seen me sobbing in my bedroom in my sunglasses last week. But I'll take the compliment.

I'm suddenly aware that the sensation of receiving a compliment from someone in a *romantic situation* feels very unfamiliar. Freddie never really gave me any. I always thought our love was just so strong it didn't need to be voiced. But now I realize that it feels nice to hear the things that someone likes about you said out loud.

I bask in warm pride for a second, then I remember I'm probably supposed to say something back. "Umm. . ." I say. "You're all right too."

He grins. I've said it before and I'll say it again, *My days, this boy is gorgeous*. We grin at each other for a moment too long. Eventually he releases my fingers and pats me on the helmet.

"Come on then, sook, shall we get you back on solid ground? I reckon you deserve a burger after all that."

I nod enthusiastically and we start climbing back down. And just when I think this is all going *pretty swimmingly*, I, quite predictably, lose my footing and my grip on the rope.

I hang on with one arm for a bit, thinking I might just save it . . . when I fall.

Obviously.

CHAPTER

SEVEN

The next day at Aimee's, she treats me like I'm a china doll that might smash at any second. I'm sitting on Aimee's big, comfy cream bed and reach for a mug on her bedside table.

"Ah, ah!" She springs up. "*Careful!*" She picks up the tea for me and puts it in my good hand.

"I can pick up a mug, thanks," I hiss.

"Cool, cool, cool." She nods. "You go, girl."

Apparently I'm so unsporty that I even need motivational quotes to help me through *picking up a mug*.

"You're as bad as Dad," I say. "It's just a sprain."

Dad did not take the news well. Last night I could feel him listening at my door to check I was still breathing (because I hear wrist injuries really affect the lungs) and this morning I heard him on the phone to the hospital at least three different times, confirming whether they could say "with total certainty" I'd live. I think he only let me out this evening because he still feels bad about what happened with Freddie.

"By the way, I spoke to Belinda," Aimee says. "Now that you're *incapacitated*, I thought it would give us a fresh angle on the please-let-Maya-stop-cleaning-loos situation, but to no avail. She is ICE COLD. She said you can use your other hand, and that if I ask her one more time she's going to fire me."

I laugh out loud. "She really is cold. Thank you for continuing to fight my corner, but it's fine; I've kind of made my peace with the cleaning. At least I get to spend the summer *near* you guys."

"I still can't believe you sprained your wrist at the assault course," Joe interjects. He is sitting in the corner, shaking his head. He sounds genuinely upset. "Ten year olds go there."

"Once again, Joe, you're not responsible. Don't worry." Aimee rolls her eyes.

Joe ignores the comment and looks at his hands.

"Oh. Of course you're not, Joe. That's stupid," I say, surprised. I had no idea he felt that way. "You weren't going to turn me into a fully-fledged athlete in a matter of hours."

"Sorry you hurt yourself," he mumbles.

"Oh my days, will you two stop?" I yell. "It's not even a fracture! It's a *sprain!*"

"OK, OK." Aimee concedes. "Enough about the wrist. How was your date?!"

I smile to myself and my heart does a little swoop in my chest. I feel a bit giddy. Adam and I had ended up spending most of our date in A&E. Which sounds like the worst date in history, but it somehow managed to be fun. It was like after I'd fallen off a climbing wall on my butt, got laughed at by a massive group of kids and had to go to hospital, the worst had already happened, so I completely relaxed. We played "catch the Malteser in your mouth" and "guess what animal I am pretending to be" and all kinds of stupid games, until my dad came to collect me. When Dad arrived in the car park, Adam had said, "Well then, bye, sook. Don't get in any more trouble on the way home." As he walked away he turned back and *winked* and I melted like the British tourist I am under his hot Australian glare.

"It was *good*." I put my good hand on my chest as I say this, and give a little sigh. "Really good. I had *so much fun*. Apart from the minor injury. And he's so . . . *easy-going*."

It's strange; I never considered myself going out with a "free-spirited backpacker", but I really liked how super chilled out and in the moment he was. He said he was just "happy to hang out" and "glad I was OK". I can't help but think Freddie would have been on his phone the whole time and then, when after all that it was just a sprain, he probably would have posted about it on social media as a joke. I always thought it was funny when he posted teasing things about everyone... But it was actually nice to feel like Adam was laughing with me, not at me and seemed to have no interest in using my splatfest as a way of getting likes. Even if Freddie was just joking.

"Are you *sure* I shouldn't cancel the others?" I double-check.

"YES! Goddamnit, M!" Aimee yells. "How many times?"

"But I think I – drum roll, please..." I hold my hands up. Joe does a fake drum roll on the table. "Thank you, Joe... I think I worked out *my new type*!"

Joe stops drum-rolling. Aimee raises her eyebrow.

"I think, with Freddie, there's *every possibility* I was focusing on things that didn't matter as much as I thought they did," I continue. "But now I know. The things that *really* matter are a) being laid-back and free-spirited, b) having an Australian accent, and c) being seriously ripped."

I bite my lip, thinking of *those arms*. I thought Aimee would be pleased with my revelation. Especially as she is an advocate for his "Hot Plate" stomach. But she throws a pillow at me and yells, "Stop putting all your eggs in one basket!"

"But what if it's the right basket?!" I defend. A boy who scales walls, works out at the gym and has seen the world... I'm practically the heart-eyed emoji just thinking about him.

"You've met him once!" Aimee retorts. "You have two other eggs to taste."

"But—"

"GO TASTE THOSE EGGS!" she shouts.

"To be fair, Maya," Joe chimes in. "I used to think poached egg was the best kind of egg, until I had scrambled with chives and cheese." He looks into the mid-distance dreamily, obviously thinking of his favourite eggs.

"I don't think you two are quite getting the expression right," I say. "Adam, Noah and Jake wouldn't be the eggs in this scenario. They'd be the baskets. Beautiful, hot baskets."

"Hush, nerd," Aimee says. "You need to stop trying to control how everything should go. You don't need to plan *absolutely everything in your life*. Just sit back and *let stuff happen*."

"But I—"

"Not another word. I'm glad you enjoyed your date with

Hot Plate, but you are NOT cancelling your date with Hot Sauce. He is coming to pick you up in three hours and that's that. Your head may yet be turned. Now, listen. . ."

I huff, still riding the roller-coaster wave of my feelings for Adam in my mind. I am still adamant my head won't get turned, but I stay quiet.

Aimee presses *play* on her speakers, which are linked to Joe's Spotify account. Music with a rage like I've never heard before fills the room. It sounds like everything I want to express when I'm having a really, really bad period, and then maybe drop my toast on the floor.

"Is this *music?*" I ask genuinely.

"Music you're a fan of." Aimee nods. "Sorry. My bad." She looks innocently up at me as if she had been totally unaware of the fact that I'd never listened to anything more ragey than Ed Sheeran.

I glower at her. We all listen for a while. . . Aimee entertains herself by headbanging and dancing with a pillow. And then, if I'm not very much mistaken, we hear Joe singing along.

". . . *are a kernel of hope, wait for them to bloom in spring. . .*" We hear him murmuring the lyrics softly.

"JOE!" Aimee shrieks. "Are you a SoC fan!!!!" She stops headbanging and stares at him, openmouthed.

"I mean, they've got a few good tracks. . ." he mumbles.

"Oh my God. You *dark horse*. Can you believe this?" She turns to me. "Joe likes intense brooding music. He's an *intense brooding man*. Who knew?"

"Shut up." Joe chucks the pillow Aimee threw at me, back at her.

After half an hour or so, Aimee's commitment really begins to wane. We decide to keep the music on "in the background" whilst Joe and Aimee challenge each other to a video game. At some point I realize the music has stopped and I've just been watching Aimee crush Joe at *Smash Bros* for the last hour.

The plan was to listen to enough songs that I'd know the words, but eventually we decide I'll just nod my head and look solemn and hopefully get away with it.

"Intense musicians don't like it when you sing along anyway, M," Aimee asserts. "They're far too brooding for that."

Definitely just trying to excuse herself for being ultimately more interested in *Smash Bros* than my love life. Which would be fine, if all of this wasn't *her fault in the first place*.

"Oh, I know, let's practise your brooding look!" Joe exclaims.

"Is it just me or is Joe way too excited about this?" Aimee asks.

Joe shoots her what I assume is his "brooding look".

We spend the next ten minutes looking broodily at each other (if you haven't tried it, act like you've got a hook in your eyebrow and something really bad-smelling under your nose).

"Do you feel prepared?" Joe asks. By this point his face is so "broody" he looks like a wizened old man.

I notice the time. Oh my days. It's five minutes until Noah arrives. I'm about to answer (no, I do not feel prepared) when there's a loud VROOOOOOM noise from the street outside. We all stop "brooding" and frown at each other. That sounds awfully like ... a motorbike?! Aimee, Joe and I all look at each other for a second and dash to the window. We crouch down by the windowsill and peep out. Surely it can't be. No. *It is.*

There's Noah, wearing skinny jeans and DMs and a leather jacket, leaning with one foot up against the side of a *giant motorbike*. He's wearing a helmet and casually holding another one in his hand.

"Of course he has a motorbike," Joe exclaims. "Of course he does. Is that a Norton?" He squints. "Of course it bloody is!"

My mouth gapes open. I'm in shock. Is he serious? A motorbike?!

"How old is he?! I thought you had to be a grown-up to ride a motorbike!"

"You only have to be seventeen," Joe says bitterly. "I asked my mums and they said a big fat no."

"Well . . . *same*," I stammer. My dad only just agreed to let me leave the house after the wrist incident. I think his heart would give out if he saw a boy turning up to get me *on a motorbike!*

He must never know.

My phone buzzes.

Hey sook, how's the wrist? Adam

"Is that him?" Aimee asks.

"No, it's Adam." I show her the screen and beam. "That's nice, isn't it?"

Aimee rips my mobile out of my hand and hits me on the head with it. "Get your head in the game, M. It's time for round two."

"Right, yeah, round two," I repeat uncertainly, looking through the window at Noah and his *actual motorbike*.

Actual. Motorbike.

"Right, I'm off, wish me luck and no more injuries," I say.

"I'm not liking your chances," Joe says, eyeing the bike.

Aimee hugs me and Joe pats me awkwardly on the head, then I head to the door. Joe and Aimee follow me.

"Um, didn't realize this was a date for four," I say.

"Yeah, Joe," Aimee pushes him backwards. And keeps on following me. Eventually I get her to leave me alone and head outside solo.

As I walk along the street Noah looks up and smiles. *Those eyes*. I feel so exposed! It's like in one glance they see inside your head and rifle through all of your thoughts. I wonder if he will be able to tell I went out with an action-loving adventure-type boy last night and am going out with a highly sensitive, kitten-rescuing pretty-boy tomorrow? Is it written all over my face?

"Hey," he says.

I scan his eyes for any knowledge that I'm a big, snakey snake. But I can't see anything.

"Hi." I wave and point at the helmet. "That for me?"

He laughs and looks embarrassed. "So, we *really don't have to*. I have a back-up plan for if you feel uncomfortable. We can walk to the station and take the train, and get a taxi the other side."

I chew the inside of my cheek. "Am I definitely old enough?" I check.

"Yes." Noah smiles. "Even under sixteens can ride pillion."

I nod. Every molecule of me is terrified to get on the back of that bike. But I felt the same way about climbing the huge wall and (even though I sprained my wrist) I did end up having a lot of fun. It was something I would never have considered doing and I'm glad I did. And even though if I had the choice, my summer would have followed my original plan – the one where I'm sitting with my "perfect" boyfriend holding hands over our tapas – I think about what Aimee said, about trying to plan *absolutely everything* and just letting some stuff in my life *happen*. I take a deep breath.

"I'm in," I say.

"Awesome." He smiles and hands me the helmet.

"Oh, wait," I add. "Is this going to be a problem?" I wave my arm, exposing my wrist support.

He frowns. "Oh *no*. What did you do? Are you OK?"

I cough, avoiding the first question. "I'm fine, it's just a sprain."

"All right, well, I think it should be fine, if you make sure both elbows are properly around me, and hold on extra tight with the other arm."

The words "extra tight" make my lungs constrict. He gets on the bike and I climb on behind him. I sit stiffly.

"Uh, you're going to have to sit a little closer," he says. "And hold a little tighter."

"Oh, um, sure." I shuffle forwards and put my arms around his waist. I'm so tense I can barely breathe. He's very *warm*. And *thin*. He's a totally different body type to Adam but, interestingly, I find myself thinking it's just as attractive. Maybe Aimee *was* right about this whole multiple eggs thing?

I hear a wolf whistle in the distance and look up to Aimee's window, where I see the top of Aimee's head bob down.

"Friend of yours?" Noah jokes. He stares up at Aimee's window for quite a long time before turning to smile at me.

"Nope, never seen her before in my life," I answer.

He starts up the engine and we zoom off into the night.

CHAPTER

EIGHT

The motorbike ride is *completely insane*. Like nothing I have ever experienced before. I genuinely feel like I'm flying.

We ride for about twenty minutes then come to a stop in a little cobbled street, outside a small church. I look up at the grey stones, long arched windows and spire silhouetted against the pink-and-orange sunset. Is he sure we're in the right place?

"Not what you were expecting?" he asks.

"Not quite," I admit.

We get off the bike. He takes off his helmet and shakes out his long fringe. He smiles down at me. One half of his face is in shadow and the other is cast in the luminous glow of the summer evening. His eyes look even darker and more intense than they do in daylight.

"Shall we?" He offers me his arm and I loop my hand through it. I feel like a *lady of high society* in a Jane Austen novel. If high-society ladies went to see heavy metal bands screaming and headbanging in converted churches.

We enter through the huge double archway. Inside the building is cool and airy, which I suppose is what makes it the perfect place for a gig on a hot summer's night. We're early but people are already milling around in groups waiting for the support act to start. The atmosphere in the air is electric; I can sense how much everyone in the room wants to see the band. Random people nod and shoot us "knowing looks". It's like I've happened upon the password to let myself into some sort of exclusive underground member's club. Regular, oblivious society is out there bobbing along blindly, and we're all in here, separate from the rest, united in our shared passion for this hip, alternative group. (That I'd never heard of before two days ago.)

I head to the café and I order some drinks, whilst Noah grabs us some seats in a pew at the back. A girl with her head shaved on one side and a nose ring makes eye contact with me. *This is it. This is my moment.* It's time for my best brooding look. I raise one eyebrow at her, imagine there's a fish under my nose, and slowly tilt my neck forwards.

She looks slightly perplexed for a moment, but then she nods at me! I did it! *I'm practically one of them!*

I turn back to the waiter and order our drinks. He pushes them along the counter to me with a nod. I nod back. Everyone in here is *so cool*.

"Sorry," I say to Noah as I rejoin him. "They didn't have any Fanta, only Coke. Is this OK?"

He takes it and stares at it for quite a long time.

Is the Coke OK? Is he wishing I'd got him a Sprite?! Or is he above caring about what type of sugary drink he enjoys the most and is thinking about something else entirely?! Maybe he's thinking about the state of politics, or climate change, or trying to come up with ways to end world hunger, or pondering if life after death really exists.

"Thanks," he says finally.

Or maybe he really is just thinking about Coke.

I smile at him and sip my own drink. This boy is ridiculously hard to read. I'd never imagined myself with a "mysterious" boy before. I always knew exactly what was going on in Freddie's head. It was pretty much a) food, b) laughing at random Youtube videos, c) laughing at something silly his mates had done. I thought I liked knowing what was going on in my boyfriend's head, but now I'm not so sure. I'm organized; I like to know where

I stand. I have no time for working out how other people are feeling about Coke! But Noah – with his edgy hair cut, motorbike, searching dark eyes and faraway stare – is basically the stereotypical "enigmatic love interest" of every YA novel I have ever read and I find myself *surprisingly intrigued.*

"So, your friend Aimee seemed pretty determined that you come along tonight... You must be really into SoC. What's your favourite song?" Noah asks.

My gut clenches. This is the question I had been dreading. I rack my brains for a song title. Was it "Immortal Souls Never Die"? No ... of course immortal souls wouldn't die. That's the basic premise of being "immortal". Or do bands care about such contradictions? What was another one?! "Love Like Peroxide". Or was it Carbon Monoxide? Why do all these songs sound basically *exactly the same?!*

Thankfully, long gaps in the conversation don't seem to make Noah uncomfortable. He probably thinks I have so many favourite songs I'm just having a really hard time choosing. "Erm ... 'Immortal Souls Never *Sleep*'?" I finally answer.

I search his face for a clue as to whether I passed the SoC fan test, but he gives nothing away.

"You're a fan of the old stuff, then," he comments.

"They'll play some of it, but their new material is a little different."

"That's fine," I say. *Phew.* At least I got the name of a song right. I need to change the subject, fast, so I rack my brains for what I already know about Noah. I think he said he was working about a million jobs, saving to go on a tour. "So you're in a band too, right? How much more do you need to save before you can go on tour?"

Noah nods. I can tell from the look in his eyes, and from how hard he works at Casa Nadar, that he really cares about the band. He's in there every shift he can get.

"We've nearly got enough to record our first album," he says. "And yeah, then the plan is to go around Europe. Maybe start in Germany."

We talk for a little longer about his band, until he suddenly does that spooky eye contact thing, like he's trying to read my thoughts. "So are you feeling any better this weekend?" He looks right at me, his eyes shining on me like spotlights.

I look away awkwardly, only able to handle a normal-person amount of eye contact. (Three point three seconds is considered the optimum for standard social interaction, in case you were wondering.) "Um, I'm fine."

"Really?" he presses softly. "Your friend Aimee seemed pretty worried about you."

I look at him then away again quickly. His gaze is like a laser beam.

"I . . ."

I think of Freddie and this summer, and where I was supposed to be, and where I've ended up. How I was on a straight line moving forwards and now I'm spinning in all sorts of directions on a roller coaster of different emotions . . . and we're only two weeks into the holidays.

"*Sometimes the mysteries of life are a kernel of hope; wait for them to bloom in spring or else you might never sing,*" he cuts in.

I'm about to say "Huh?" but then I realize this is probably some apt SoC lyric, so I just give him my best "brooding look" and pretend to think about it for a while, and he seems satisfied.

We chat through the support band and, although I'm never *completely sure* what he's thinking or feeling, I do get to know him a little. It's very different from getting to know Adam, who's such an open book. Although they're not as different as I thought . . . I assumed cool, mysterious types didn't have any sense of humour, but he ends up making me laugh several times. Not in the same silly, charming way as Adam – more in a cutting, dry way that comes out of nowhere – but he's funny.

OMD. I realize I haven't replied to Adam. Can I

do that on a date with another guy?! Should I even be thinking about Adam right now?

Thankfully, the band comes on before I can panic too much. Noah takes my hand and it's like a little current of electricity runs through my fingers. We get up and move towards where the crowd has gathered.

The band are *so good*. It doesn't matter that I wasn't a fan of them before; I get so wrapped up in their music and in the atmosphere of the crowd. Plus, I sort of know a few songs now, from Joe playing them earlier. As they perform I can hear Joe singing along in my mind and try to join in for the bits I remember.

Noah's face lights up during their set. It's the one time in the evening where I really can tell what he's feeling. Neither of us are focusing on anything else but the music and dancing. People sway around us, and every so often I look up to the beautiful converted church ceiling, and the last of the daylight flowing in the stained-glass windows, and I feel completely alive.

One minute Noah is beside me, and then suddenly he's raised up above the crowd, on the shoulders of four random people. He smiles down and offers me his hand. Does he want *me* to crowd-surf? Because I can safely say now that is *never going to happen*.

But then everyone around me is giving me

encouraging looks. One girl is pointing upwards. Another is leaning down so I can climb on her back. *Oh my days.* Am I really going to do this?! Is this what's known as "peer pressure"? I don't think I've ever had enough friends to have really been exposed to it before, but suddenly I feel the overwhelming urge to do what everyone wants.

I clamber on the girl's shoulders. The group cheers. Noah reaches over and pats me on the back. For a moment it feels like the right decision. For a moment.

And then I'm catapulted up into the air and the girl totters under my weight. Unlike Noah, who seemed to float seamlessly towards the skies with the grace of a ballerina, I wobble from side to side. I can feel the girl weaken underneath me, which is no surprise, given how tall I am and how tiny she is. It's like a giraffe trying to ride a fawn. I feel as though she genuinely might shatter as her body shudders beneath my weight. I reach out a hand to stop myself falling and it lands on her friend's shoulder, who scowls at me and mouths "Are you OK, babe?" at her small friend. All right, *"babe"!!!* They seem to have forgotten it was them who *told me to get up here!*

I'm passed on to the next person, who at least seems a bit sturdier. But no one ever warned me how much crowd-surfing *hurts*. I'm being prodded and poked, and this really wasn't a good idea with my sprained wrist and . . . is someone *UNDOING MY SHOES?!*

I peer down towards my feet, trying to get a good look, but the crowd is too huge. Some *underhanded crook* is taking my shoes and there is nothing I can do about it!! I feel the first one slip off. And then the second. And then my socks!!! Why my SOCKS?! Oh, this just takes the BISCUIT!

"THIEF! THIEF!" I yell. But no one can hear me. Noah's already sailed off in a different direction. The boy next to me pumps his fist upwards and shouts, "YEAH!" clearly thinking I'm just impassioned by the music.

Eventually, once I've been sufficiently mauled, I am placed down at the front of the crowd battered and barefoot. The floor is *so cold on my feet*. I rush immediately up to a bouncer.

"Excuse me," I say. "Some *unscrupulous criminal* has stolen my shoes."

He just looks at my feet and laughs. How helpful.

Someone taps me on the shoulder. It's Noah. I'm about to rage to him about my shoes, but he looks so pleased to have found me again that I'm caught off guard. He takes my hand. Then the angry song comes crashing to an end and a single piano note plays. A softer melody fills the air and my temper drifts off with it. Noah stares deep into my eyes.

"You lost your shoes." He finally notices and points at my toes.

Shoes? What are shoes?

"You can't walk back through the crowd; your feet will get annihilated."

He pats his shoulder, gesturing for me to put my arms around his neck. I lean forward and he bends down, looping his arms under my knees and scooping me up into the air. He carries me through the crowd and, *oh wow*, he is stronger than he looks. My face is right next to his neck. It's a *very attractive neck*.

I think I might be giddy.

He puts me down right at the back by the pews, where we were sitting earlier, where the floor is wooden and less freezing. He holds out his arm again, leaning forward, and speaks in my ear. His breath is hot on the side of my face.

"Care to dance?" he asks.

I nod.

He puts his arms around my waist. I put my arms around his shoulders, and we draw in closer and start moving side to side. The whole room is swaying in time to the slow, beautiful song. I've never slow-danced before. Well, I once slow-danced with Aimee when we were acting out a scene from *Pride and Prejudice*. But I've never slow-danced with an *actual boy*. I don't think any woman has since 1886. I may well be the only one in modern times.

"You're interesting, Maya," he says in my ear. "You really feel things. I can tell."

I am definitely feeling *all the things* right now.

We keep dancing until the song finishes. When it ends, he lifts me back up and carries me out to his motorbike. It's *very romantic*, even when he has to wrap plastic bags around my feet to protect them for the ride home. The whole journey back, that last song is still playing in my head. Later that night I dance around my room to it, still shoeless.

Aimee was right, I think to myself guiltily as I sway back and forth. My head has been turned *the full one eighty degrees*.

CHAPTER

nine

The next morning I wake up to two different messages.

Had fun last night. Sorry about your shoes! :/ Nx

**Can't wait for tomorrow, my address is 6
Hadley Drive. Jake x**

And I still haven't replied to Adam's message. My
question is, how do serial daters ever get anything
else done? Who on earth has the time for this sort of
relationship maintenance?!

"You never were very good at multitasking," says
Aimee. We're in my kitchen and she's chopping up some
mushrooms in one hand and some parsley in the other.

"Unlike *moi*." She grins and brandishes the two knives at me with a flourish.

It's my third and final date tonight, with Jake. He suggested we cook a *"coq au vin"* together (again, had to google it) before taking Stefan out for a long walk.

"Aimee, *please!*" Joe cries. "You're making me nervous! You're going to lose a finger!"

"Shhh, Joe," she says. "I'm teaching Maya the art of dating. Just imagine this parsley is Hot Plate. And these mushrooms are Hot Sauce. And this chicken is Hot Dog. How would you feel if you'd only tried the mushrooms and the parsley, and you said all right, these both taste pretty good, I'll just keep eating these ... but you hadn't tasted the chicken yet? You'd never know you were missing out on the BEST bit."

"Another dubious comparison, because surely in a *coq au vin* I'd be trying them all at the same time," I say.

"*Now* you're talking," Aimee says.

"Ames, you sound like a pervy middle-aged mum," says Joe. "Just chop these shallots."

Aimee flings a mushroom at Joe's head but ultimately obeys him. "I still don't get why *you're* learning to make a *coq au vin*," she says. "Surely Jake will be cooking for you?"

"Because if I am going on this date, which I am still

unsure about," I reply, "I am *at least* going to help, and I do not want to make a fool of myself."

"Anyway, cooking is fun." Joe grins. He's wearing my dad's flowery pinny and has assumed position as head chef. Dad and Joe both *love* food (making it and eating it). I considered asking Dad for help preparing for this evening, but he would've asked too many questions about my sudden interest in cooking. So I pleaded with Aimee and Joe to come over and help me do a test run when he went to work.

"I say sit back and let him serve you tasty food." Aimee rubs her hands together.

"I don't want to take advantage. I'm telling you it's pointless," I say. "I'll go tonight to please you, but I've made up my mind. Hands down. I worked it out last night when I was dancing with Noah. *Forget* accents and muscles. The most important things to me in a boyfriend are a) creativity, b) ability to slow-dance, c) being in possession of a motorbike."

Aimee bursts out laughing. But I'm deadly serious. My brain is too full from thinking about last night's date with Noah and his enigmatic gaze and ambition and talent and ... well, he can *play me like his guitar,* is all I'm saying. *Sigh*.

"Maya." Joe clicks his fingers. "Please concentrate on the task at hand." He waves a bottle of oil in my face.

"All right, all right." I take it from him.

"OK, Maya..." Joe says slowly. "Now put a splash of oil in this pan..."

"Joe," I say. "I'm not a child. You can talk at a normal speed."

"Well, I don't know, M... In the last two days you have sprained your wrist falling off a climbing wall intended for children and lost your shoes."

"Man's got a point," Aimee remarks.

"OK, OK." I snatch the oil from him (with my good hand). I feel like it would be petty to remind him of all the academic achievements that demonstrate I'm not quite as air-headed as the events of the last two days would imply.

I pour the oil into the pan and gently fry the shallots, regularly stirring them. Joe watches my every move closely. Aimee stands in the corner doing an interpretive "parsley dance". (It's quite distracting and bizarre).

We put in the garlic and the Cognac for the "glaze". Then we put in the chicken and the red wine. It's all very fancy but not overly complicated. I think Joe was bigging it up a bit, to be honest. Almost like he *wanted* to spend his entire afternoon showing me how to chop onions. When we lower the heat to simmer for an hour he says:

"Have you got all that, Maya? Shall I message you the instructions?"

"No need, no need," I say. "I extracted DNA from a cell all by myself, Joe. I got *one hundred percent* on my last biology exam. I'm sure I can remember how to make a glorified chicken casserole. But thanks."

"All right, all right." Joe holds his hands up.

"Yeah, don't mansplain, Joe, God," Aimee jokes.

"How am I *mansplaining?!*" Joe chokes. "I'm just explaining!"

"You're a man." Aimee shrugs.

"You explain things way more assertively than I do!" Joe cries. "How am I ever supposed to. . ."

"Hush, Joe, I'm obviously joking." Aimee grins.

Joe murmurs something under his breath about being best friends with two girls.

"All right, sorry guys, I've got to go. Dance class calls." Aimee jumps down from the counter. "Have you got it from here?"

"You mean without your interpretive parsley dance? I think we'll be fine," Joe mutters.

"I don't like it when you're sassy, Joe." Aimee sticks her tongue out. "It doesn't suit you." Eventually she heads out, calling, "Bye, guys! Have fun with Hot Dog, M!"

We hear her slam the door. Once it's just Joe and me, there's an instant lapse in conversation. It's not awkward as such, just . . . unusual. It's funny. . . Joe and I have been friends for a year now, but we don't generally spend time without Aimee. Joe will ask Aimee to hang out alone, but never me. I sometimes wonder if he secretly fancies her deep down. He probably wouldn't even be here unless Aimee hadn't dragged him along. I suddenly feel guilty.

"You can go too if you want?" I offer. "You must be really bored of prepping me for various dates."

"I wouldn't say bored." Joe smiles. Then he suddenly looks worried. "I mean, unless you want me to go? Sorry, I should have thought, you probably want to curl your hair or bathe in lavender salts or something. . . Now that Aimee's gone, I mean, I should have thought. . . Look, I'll just run through the last instructions with you, yeah? To make the mashed potatoes you just—"

"Joe!" I say.

He stops rambling.

"Put down the potato. I'd like you to stay."

"Oh." Joe grins. "Then I will stay."

"Bathe in lavender salts?" I ask.

He shrugs. "My mums and sisters always seem to be bathing in lavender salts."

I smile. "You totally do too, don't you?"

He laughs and coughs at the same time. "Ahhh. . . I may have tried them once. So, we've got some time until the *coq au vin* is ready. . ." He looks at his phone.

"Sorry, I don't have any video games." I shrug. "Dad says they're a waste of time. I think that's because he spent the entire eighties playing Pac-Man."

"That's fair." Joe laughs.

"I have board games, though?" I offer.

"Oh, ace!" Joe says. With anyone else I might think they were being sarcastic, but I know Joe is genuine.

We go to Dad's ancient board game collection and Joe *oohs* and *aahs* over it. Finally he pulls out Operation.

"You want to be a doctor, don't you?" Joe waves it around. "Excellent practice."

"Exactly like the real thing," I laugh. "And *yes*. I do. At least, that's always been the plan..."

We lay out the board, i.e. the picture of the shirtless man in pink, heart-covered shorts. Joe goes first and tries to pull out the guy's "wish bone" without hitting the edge.

"So is that not still the plan—" BZZZZ. "Damn!" He puts the tweezers down. "You don't sound sure? I've always thought that's what you really wanted."

"Um. . ." I go in for the "spare ribs". "I don't know. It was. But I've been wondering recently if I need a new plan."

We're quiet for a moment as I hover the tweezers over the guy's chest.

"Do you mind if I, er, ask why?"

"Something Dad said about him and Mum working too hard when they were young. I guess I wonder if that was part of why it didn't work out. YESSS! Got the ribs!"

"Damn you!" Joe looks intently at the game. He doesn't respond to my comment for a while and I start wondering if he's going to reply at all.

"Sorry, was that TMI?" I suddenly worry. I haven't shared this with anyone yet, even Aimee. I don't even think I've really interrogated the thought myself before. I'm not sure why I blurted it out.

"No, not at all." Joe keeps looking at the game. He takes the tweezers and goes in for the "Adam's apple". I feel a ramble coming. "I was just thinking ... that you can't know how things are going to go. I mean, yeah, you might work less and have more time for a relationship, but it might not be the right relationship. Or you might work super hard and become a doctor and then meet your super-hard-working doctor husband and have little doctor babies. I suppose this is my long way of saying just because something happened for your parents doesn't mean it's going to happen the same to you."

I let Joe's words settle for a moment and realize, in his own rambly way, he's a-hundred-per-cent right. I feel a warm sense of reassurance. Of course I want to be a doctor. I've always wanted to be a doctor, and I shouldn't let anything stop me.

"There's no way of knowing what's going to happen, so don't try and plan for it, basically," he continues. BZZZZZZZ. "Damnit!!!"

I laugh. "I think I'm slowly learning that."

Joe smirks and looks me in the eye. "You mean dating three mega dream hunks wasn't on your carefully constructed agenda?"

"Mega dream hunks? Do *you* want to go out with them, Joe?" I nudge him.

He smiles. "Shut up and get your funny bone."

I lean in and get it no problem.

"I swear this thing is rigged," Joe mutters.

After playing Operation we eat the *coq au vin* (which is *amazing*). Then I notice the time.

"Oh, I have to go, I'm going to be late."

"Already?" For a second I wonder if Joe looks almost disappointed. But then the expression passes. He clears his throat. "I mean, I know you said you can handle it, but are you quite sure you're ready to eat another *coq au vin* straight after this one? That's a lot of chicken and wine. Eating a balanced diet, you know, a wide variety of foods in the correct proportions, is important to maintaining your health. I mean . . . especially for a future doctor."

"I'm sure I'll survive. Thanks, Joe." I smile.

We clear up the plates and head to the front door. Joe stands on the path whilst I lock up.

"All right, bye then, M." He leans in and gives me a hug.

"Bye, Joe. See you later on." I hug him back. I'm not sure why I feel a bit sad to be leaving. It's not like I don't see Aimee and Joe *every single day*. Watching Joe's retreating back, I try to shake off the feeling. I'm probably just on edge about my third date in a week (!) and wanting the security blanket of my mates. Would it be socially acceptable to bring Joe with me? I can't imagine my date being anywhere near as comfortable as the last hour has been.

I sigh as Joe turns the corner and disappears out of sight. Time for date number three.

CHAPTER

TEN

I stand outside the address Jake gave me. It's just down the road from Casa Nadar. I can hear the music, laughter and splashing from where I'm standing. For a moment I just breathe in the balmy summer air, but as I *cannot stand* latecomers, eventually I move towards the front door and knock.

And come face to face with Belinda's boobs. She's wearing a top that shows them off, and even though I don't like her, I have to admit she's looking like a *queen*.

I take a step backwards. "Am I at the wrong house?" I blink.

"Oh, I meant to leave before you got here." Belinda looks me up and down and grimaces.

All right.

"So I am at the right house?" I repeat.

"Unfortunately." She steps aside to let me in, then goes to check her appearance in the hallway mirror.

"So, you're Jake's..."

"Cousin, yeah, well done. I thought you were smart? Don't you want to be a doctor or something?"

"I just..." I grit my teeth. "If you're here, why does Jake have to look after the dog?"

"Oh, is *that* why Jake told you he was here for the summer?" Belinda raises her eyebrows. "I thought he was here to see a certain person, but who knows, maybe it *was* about the dog."

A "certain" person? What person?! What's she talking about? *And Jake's cousin is Belinda?!* This is all far too much new information to process at once. I consider turning around and heading back down the path, but Jake appears in the doorway to the kitchen.

Oh, that face. I'd forgotten that face.

"Maya!" He beams. His expression is so open and friendly.

And cute.

I look between him and Belinda. It's funny but I can't see any family resemblance – in looks *or* personality.

"Are you trying to work out why we don't look alike?"

Belinda asks. "I'm adopted, actually, no need to be so rude about it."

I open my mouth. "Oh, I..."

"JOKING!" She cackles. I think that's the only time I've ever seen her laugh. Apart from that time she scored a goal after tackling Angelina Simons to the ground and Angelina cried.

"Ha ha," I say weakly.

"Well, I'll just get out of your hair. Leave you two lovebirds alone."

So awkward.

"Thanks, B, love you byeeeeeee." Jake ushers her out of the house. When the door closes he turns to me. "I'm sorry. She can be..."

"Don't worry," I say, thinking of the sprout mac 'n' cheese my dad made the other day. Families are always interesting.

What was that about this mystery person though?

Jake leads me into the kitchen, where all the ingredients for the *coq au vin* are laid out.

"So I thought I'd make you a *coq au vin*." He gestures to the counter. "Sit back, relax..."

"Oh, I don't mind helping," I say. "I make *coq au vin all the time*."

"Really?" Jake raises one eyebrow.

"Yep. *Coq au vin* this, *coq au vin* that, I'm all over the coq au vin. Just say the word *coq*, think Maya."

I suddenly realize how the word "*coq*" sounds when you say it out loud.

"I mean..." I start.

Bless Jake, he doesn't laugh at my slip-up; he just breezes past it and hands me a knife. I forgot how sweet he seemed when we first met. My mind is still *occasionally* drifting to my last date, and the one before... Surely, this date cannot be as swoon-worthy as they were? But for the first time all weekend, I'm actually glad I agreed to this date.

We start chopping all the vegetables (which, I note with satisfaction, he has laid out in order of when we will need each of them. *Wait. Hold the phone. Forget everything I said about the other guys. Do we have a winner?!* "Calm down, Maya." I hear Aimee's voice in my head. "Being mutually hyper organized does not equal love.")

"So, you're into cooking?" He looks down at the vegetables on the counter with a small smile as I lose my grip on a shallot. It goes rolling on to the floor.

"Uh, my dad is, in his own way..." I pick up the shallot and carry on chopping. I can still hear Joe's instructions in my ear as I expertly slice everything up.

"Good man," Jake says.

"So, did you always want to be a vet?" I ask.

"Pretty much, ever since I was little and found a half-crushed butterfly in our garden and couldn't stop crying. I tried so hard to save its wing. I might start crying now just thinking about it." Jake laughs and wipes a mock tear from his eye. "Not a very masculine thing to admit, is it?"

I don't know, but thinking about him saving that little butterfly, my heart starts fluttering like one. Freddie would *never* have admitted to crying. He didn't really show emotions all that much. I thought I liked that, but thinking about Jake getting all worked up about little animals. I am suddenly getting *very hot*. And it's not just the heat of the kitchen.

"So yeah." Jake's still talking. *Must pay attention.* "I'm just studying this summer basically, and looking after Stefan, of course. The books are my theoretical practice and Stefan my actual."

I laugh.

"And what about you? Did I hear Belinda say you want to be a doctor?"

"Yep," I answer. "Both my parents are doctors. And I have an 'unnatural fascination with the human body', as my best friend Aimee puts it. But it's a lot of work."

"Nah, you'll be fine. I knew you were super smart as

soon as I met you." Jake looks up from his mushrooms to shoot me a dazzling beam.

Swoon. My heart starts fluttering again.

We go on talking for ages like this, about our dreams for the future. As he talks, something about his passion for helping animals seems to further ignite my passion for helping people. I've never met someone who seems to *care* so much about others. He doesn't have a bad word to say about anyone, and the way he sees the best in people is infectious. (I suppose you'd have to see the best in people, being related to Belinda.)

I never pictured myself with someone so sensitive. It's not like I ever set out to date someone *insensitive*, but I suppose I always assumed someone too sensitive would be . . . boring? But Jake isn't boring at all.

Our conversation is interrupted by loud barking.

"Sounds like someone's awake and grumpy." Jake leaps up. "Be one minute. Can you start the glaze? Just. . ."

"Jake, Jake." I hold my hands up. "What did I say before about *coq*? *I'm the expert.*"

OMD. Nooo. Another slip. Even Jake has to stifle a laugh at that one as he walks away. Note to self: *stop using the word coq in sentences unless immediately followed by au vin!!*

What happens next happens so quickly, I'm not sure how I manage it. I shake the pan like Joe taught me, back and forth, only I shake the chicken pan instead of the glaze. (Hindsight, wonderful thing). A bit of sizzling chicken goes flying towards the glaze pan and rolls down one side, creating a pathway of oil directly beside the flame of the gas ring. I watch the little purple flame creep closer and closer until it rushes up the oil, towards the pan filled with booze.

WHOOOSH.

OMD. OMD. What do I do. OMD OMD OMD. The pan is on fire!!!

THE PAN IS ON FIRE!!!!!!!!!!!!!

I rush around the room for a minute, opening random drawers. I'm not sure what I'm looking for because all rational thoughts have flown out of my head. I grab a spoon and hold it up towards the fire.

"STOP, FLAMES!" I yell, like the spoon is a wand.

Nothing happens. Obviously.

OMD OMD OMD OMD OMD. I'm going to *burn Jake's house down.* Shall I call 999 for help?! No. That's too embarrassing. Surely I can fix this. Pretend I meant to do this? Say I was doing that flambé thing that I heard Joe and Dad talking about once?! Or at least die in the fire so I *never have to admit that it was me?!?!*

I stand looking solemnly at the flames for a second,

spoon raised in one hand. I almost feel poetic. Like a captain about to go down with their ship.

Then I hear a voice from the doorway. "What the. . ." Jake is back, holding Stefan, staring wide-eyed at the fire on the hob. Then a loud, piercing sound shrieks through the house. For a moment I think this is the sound of death coming for me but it turns out to be the fire alarm.

Water tips down from the ceiling. Jake's family have, apparently quite rightly, installed indoor sprinklers. The fire fizzles out. We stand still, looking at each other for a few moments. Stefan whines.

Jake seems lost for words. "What were you doing with that spoon?" he asks.

I think for a moment, looking sideways at the spoon. Can I possibly style this out? "Have you never seen someone do a classic *flambé de cuillière*?"

Jake smiles. He looks even prettier when he's drenched. His hair sticks to the side of his face, a drop of water rolls down his cheek and, ahem, I can see through his shirt. "Shall we go for that walk?" he asks. "After, erm, cleaning up, obviously. . ." He looks nervously around him.

"Obviously," I say, thinking that his diligence makes me like him even more.

*

We spend a good half an hour making sure the kitchen is spotless, and mopping up the water from the fire alarm, before putting Stefan on his lead. Jake is so lovely that, on the way to the park, he barely mentions the fact that I nearly burned his house to a crisp. I think briefly of one time I spilled my drink all over myself and Freddie made a big joke out of it to everyone. I always told myself it was helpful for me, like how a good friend always tells you when you've got something in your teeth, but now I'm not so sure.

"So, did your week improve?" He gazes at me. He's referring to my crying in the men's toilets, but he doesn't say it directly. So thoughtful.

"It did," I say.

"Glad to hear it." He smiles. And even though we don't know each other very well, I believe he *is* genuinely glad to hear it.

I was only really saying my week had improved to be polite, but as soon as I say it out loud I realize it's true. I haven't properly thought about Freddie in *days*. I mean, he's crossed my mind, but I haven't been scrolling through his Instagram or obsessing over what he and Lydia might be doing. Which is strange, given that I spent every waking moment of the past year thinking about him.

CHAPTER

ELEVEN

Aimee hasn't stopped rolling her eyes since she sat down. I'm starting to find her being up on her little lifeguard chair whilst I talk to her from down below, like a lowly servant, *really irritating*. "So let me get this straight, on one date you fell off a wall, on another you lost your shoes, then you nearly burned a guy's house down, and they all still like you?!"

"Yes."

"And you like them all back?"

"Yes."

Last night after getting home, I tried to work out how my head could possibly have been turned *a third time*. Another one-eighty? That doesn't even make sense! If that was the case, wouldn't it be back at the same spot?!

We stroll through the trees and I take a big breath of evening summer air into my lungs. It's so hot and peaceful. This must genuinely be the most glorious weather I've ever experienced in my life.

Jake takes Stefan off the lead. He darts across the grass barking and we watch him run around with reckless abandon.

"I wish I could still run like that," I comment. "Like a little kid playing chase."

"Can't you?" Jake challenges.

"You're on," I say. And I run. I run and run and run until I have no breath left in me. I can hear Jake coming up beside me and watch him overtake. I collapse in a heap on the floor.

"OK, Belinda was right about me," I wheeze. "I can't run to save my life."

"Don't worry," Jake says. For a minute I think he's genuinely comforting me about my inability to run, but then he says, "You can't be as good at everything as you are at *flambé de cuillière*." And I think I like him even more.

We lie on our backs, drying off in the last of the sun.

"Want to see something amazing?" Jake asks, propping himself up on one arm.

More amazing than your eyes? I think to myself. For

a minute I panic that I've said it out loud, but thankfully I haven't.

"Yes," I manage, as I sit up.

Jake whistles to Stefan, who dutifully bounds over. He gets out his phone and pulls up Taylor Swift's Spotify page.

"Meet the world's biggest Taylor Swift fan," Jake says, hitting play on "You Need To Calm Down".

As soon as Stefan hears it, his ears prick up. He barks and stands on his hind legs.

"NO WAY!" I scream.

Jake points his arm to the right and Stefan starts shuffling as directed, in time to the music. And then to the left. Then Jake moves his finger in a circle and Stefan, keeping his bottom on the floor, shuffles round in a circle.

It is hands down the best thing I have ever seen in my life.

Then Jake clicks his fingers and Stefan stops abruptly, looking stumped. Jake laughs.

"We haven't quite perfected the bow yet, have we, buddy? But we'll get there. WELL DONE, STEFAN!" Jake claps and throws him a treat.

"Oh my days... That was..."

I'm in awe. This is *clearly* what I need in a boyfriend,

a) openness and kindness, b) the ability to cook dog that can dance to Taylor Swift. It occurs to this is date number three, and all of these boys different and amazing traits – completely differe each other, and even more different from Freddie. like a long time since I plotted to land that seat him in biology.

Jake smiles and leans towards me as he turns Swift off. I can smell his aftershave and preten inhaling the grass. Stefan barks and runs in betwee and Jake grabs him. I am watching this incredibly p boy wrestling with his incredibly cute puppy and it' most perfect moment. I couldn't have made it up. *heart.* It melts like a slushy left out in the sun.

But suddenly, as I watch them for a few mom more, all my boy-smelling, dog-hugging chill tu panic.

I've just had my third date... And I *litera them all.*

CHAPTER

ELEVEN

Aimee hasn't stopped rolling her eyes since she sat down. I'm starting to find her being up on her little lifeguard chair whilst I talk to her from down below, like a lowly servant, *really irritating*. "So let me get this straight, on one date you fell off a wall, on another you lost your shoes, then you nearly burned a guy's house down, and they all still like you?!"

"Yes."

"And you like them all back?"

"Yes."

Last night after getting home, I tried to work out how my head could possibly have been turned *a third time*. Another one-eighty? That doesn't even make sense! If that was the case, wouldn't it be back at the same spot?!

a) openness and kindness, b) the ability to cook, and c) a dog that can dance to Taylor Swift. It occurs to me that this is date number three, and all of these boys possess different and amazing traits – completely different from each other, and even more different from Freddie. It feels like a long time since I plotted to land that seat next to him in biology.

Jake smiles and leans towards me as he turns Taylor Swift off. I can smell his aftershave and pretend I'm inhaling the grass. Stefan barks and runs in between us, and Jake grabs him. I am watching this incredibly pretty boy wrestling with his incredibly cute puppy and it's the most perfect moment. I couldn't have made it up. *My heart*. It melts like a slushy left out in the sun.

But suddenly, as I watch them for a few moments more, all my boy-smelling, dog-hugging chill turns to panic.

I've just had my third date... And I *literally liked them all*.

a minute I panic that I've said it out loud, but thankfully I haven't.

"Yes," I manage, as I sit up.

Jake whistles to Stefan, who dutifully bounds over. He gets out his phone and pulls up Taylor Swift's Spotify page.

"Meet the world's biggest Taylor Swift fan," Jake says, hitting play on "You Need To Calm Down".

As soon as Stefan hears it, his ears prick up. He barks and stands on his hind legs.

"NO WAY!" I scream.

Jake points his arm to the right and Stefan starts shuffling as directed, in time to the music. And then to the left. Then Jake moves his finger in a circle and Stefan, keeping his bottom on the floor, shuffles round in a circle.

It is hands down the best thing I have ever seen in my life.

Then Jake clicks his fingers and Stefan stops abruptly, looking stumped. Jake laughs.

"We haven't quite perfected the bow yet, have we, buddy? But we'll get there. WELL DONE, STEFAN!" Jake claps and throws him a treat.

"Oh my days... That was..."

I'm in awe. This is *clearly* what I need in a boyfriend,

We stroll through the trees and I take a big breath of evening summer air into my lungs. It's so hot and peaceful. This must genuinely be the most glorious weather I've ever experienced in my life.

Jake takes Stefan off the lead. He darts across the grass barking and we watch him run around with reckless abandon.

"I wish I could still run like that," I comment. "Like a little kid playing chase."

"Can't you?" Jake challenges.

"You're on," I say. And I run. I run and run and run until I have no breath left in me. I can hear Jake coming up beside me and watch him overtake. I collapse in a heap on the floor.

"OK, Belinda was right about me," I wheeze. "I can't run to save my life."

"Don't worry," Jake says. For a minute I think he's genuinely comforting me about my inability to run, but then he says, "You can't be as good at everything as you are at *flambé de cuillière*." And I think I like him even more.

We lie on our backs, drying off in the last of the sun.

"Want to see something amazing?" Jake asks, propping himself up on one arm.

More amazing than your eyes? I think to myself. For

Which it definitely isn't... How can I be facing not one, not two, but *three* different ways at once?! I have a *revolving neck!!!*

"You don't have any inkling at all about which one you might like best?" Aimee prods.

"No." My stomach twists with guilt and nerves. I think I need one of those giant boxes of Jaffa cakes to soothe me.

"For God's sake, Maya!"

"What?!" I shriek. "You told me to date them all! 'Get to know them', you said!"

She shrugs. "I just figured you're so picky that at least two of them would do something wrong. You once said you'd never date Andy Sumner because he breathed too loudly."

"OK, I still stand by that," I shudder. "Heavy breathing is a genuine concern, but all these boys breathe at the appropriate volume!"

"All right ... chill, chill. There must be something we can base this decision on." She sips her special virgin colada smoothie that Noah made her. "OK, so... Hot Plate's the fun, chilled one with the ridiculous body, Hot Sauce's the mysterious cool one with hidden depths, and Hot Dog's the sensitive one with the brains?"

"I mean, if we're being *very basic* about it," I say.

"All right, so. . . They all tick different boxes. Got it. But what's the most important box?"

"Ehm, I don't know. I never pictured myself with *any of these guys*. These ticks are all new to me!"

Aimee slurps as she gets to the end of her drink. "Freddie was a bit of an empty box, I'll give you that."

I think that's a little harsh. Freddie ticked *loads of my boxes*. Like, being funny, and popular. . . I just didn't think that there were so many other boxes a person could tick!

"OK, I say go for Fun Adam. I mean, I know you have *moi,* obviously, but you need all the fun you can get, M. It takes *seven years* to train to be a doctor, and then you'll actually be a doctor which, by the sounds of it, means you'll never have any fun ever again. You'll be too busy saving people's lives and all that."

I bite my lip. "Yeah, I hear you. It's not like I didn't have fun with Noah and Jake, though. Just different kinds of fun. Noah is really witty. And Jake is fun in a . . . childish, innocent kind of way?"

Aimee nods. "All right. Go for Sensitive Jake then. You could use some kindness after Empty Box."

"Is that Freddie's new name?"

"I rather like it." Aimee smirks.

"I could. . . But, I don't know. It's not like Adam and

Noah aren't sensitive. Adam really opened up to me about his family. And Noah's *a musician*."

"All right." Aimee says flatly. "Ding ding ding, through process of elimination we have a winner. . . Mysterious Noah. From what I hear, long-term relationships are basically boredom and wanting to snog other people, so maybe never really knowing what he's thinking will keep you entertained."

She sounds more half-hearted than she did suggesting Adam or Jake. She must be getting very bored of all my antics.

"They're all leaving at the end of the summer anyway." I shrug. "I'm not looking for a long-term relationship."

"OK, OK, I've got it." Aimee makes one last-ditch attempt. "The really important question. Which one makes you into a *proper melt?*"

"A what?" I blink.

"You know, makes you go all soft, sappy, silly? Like you're melting?"

I think for a moment. I was swept off my feet on every date. I mean, who wouldn't be by each of those guys?

"All of them?" I answer honestly.

Aimee sighs. "Well, you just eliminated *none* of your men. But it will probs be fine. Cool, cool, cool." She leans back in her chair, flicking her hand to signal the conversation is over.

"You don't really mean that, do you?" I whine.

"You don't really want my help."

"I do, I do, please help me!" I tug at her leg pleadingly. "Aimee, you are my queen, and I am but a lowly servant, *please help me!!!*"

In the middle of begging I see the most terrifying sight. At the entrance Noah, Adam and Jake all walk in at the same time. Adam in his jokey Hawaiian shirt. Jake in his classic white tee. Noah in all black. (Even in the blinding hot sun. I wonder if he ever overheats? *So not the point right now.*)

...They are not supposed to all be here at the same time!!! Noah usually finishes his shift just as Adam comes to teach his lessons, and Jake usually swims early in the morning! Oh my days, what if one of them shows affection to me in front of the others? Or publicly references our date? My multiple get-to-know-ery is going to be *exposed*!

Visions of Adam putting his arm around me in front of Noah and Jake flood my mind. Or Noah grabbing my hand and pushing a virgin colada smoothie across the counter with a fierce, impassioned stare whilst Adam and Jake stand at the café frowning. Or Jake giving me a deep, too-long hug as Adam and Noah wonder what's going on.

This cannot be happening.

Aimee whistles and leans further back in her chair, like she's settling in for a show.

"AIMEE. WHAT DO I DO?!" I quietly scream.

She cackles. "Run."

I take Aimee's advice. One minute later I am *sprinting* down the hallway to the locker rooms. I look around me frantically for an escape and spot the supply cupboard where Joe pulled the hula hoops from (and where I presume Belinda keeps her unending supply of toilet bleach just for me).

I shut the door and lean against it. I close my eyes, breathing in, and out, in, and out. I know I can't stay in here for ever, but hopefully long enough that Jake will have his swim and leave and Adam and Noah will be too busy doing their jobs to notice me.

OMD. What if they all need to get changed, and start talking in the locker room? That's what boys do, right?! It's not called "locker room talk" for nothing! What if they all get chatting about this girl they're seeing and then *all realize it's the same person.*

OK, breathe. I can hear Aimee's voice in my head.

"They probably have other things to talk about to strangers than you, Maya."

I've still got my eyes closed when I hear a rustle. Immediately, my eyes fly open ... to a terrible sight. Belinda. In her bikini. Putting something see-through and squishy into her bra. Something that I know instantly is a silicone enhancer because me and Aimee used to shove her mum's ones down our bras when we were twelve.

I remain *veeery ... quiet. ... Please don't hear me please don't hear me please don't hear me please don't hear me please don't hear me.*

She's wearing earphones and dancing around, her long, glossy ponytail swishing side to side. This must be why she didn't hear me enter in the first place, so if I can juuust open the door and slip out the same way...

No. I can't do that. The boys might be out there.

I'M TRAPPED IN A LIVING NIGHTMARE.

I dither for a few more seconds, but Belinda turns before I can decide what to do. Her hand is still down one bikini bra cup. Her eyes settle on me. First she blushes and looks shocked. Her mouth hangs open. She quickly pulls her hand away from her silicone enhancements and pulls out her earphones. Her eyes narrow and she scowls darkly.

I gulp.

"*What* are you doing?!" she hisses.

"Hiding from three very gorgeous men who all want to date me?" I whisper.

"Sure." She snorts.

She doesn't have to sound *quite* so unconvinced!

"*Spying* on me, more like." She carries on. "Well *fine*. If it will stop you blabbing about this" – she waves a silicone chicken fillet wildly – "then you can have that lifeguard role you've been begging me for. OK? You can even start today. At least I'll finally have Aimee off my back; she hasn't stopped going on about it since you started."

"I wasn't..."

"But if you breathe a *word* of this to *anybody*." She comes up close to me and points her finger in my face. I can smell her perfume mixed with her perfect fake tan, that I only know is fake because she has it all year round. "*You* will be face down in that pool, got it?"

She looks livid. I mean, she always looks livid, but this is livid even for Belinda. I want to tell her that I couldn't care less if she enhances her breasts or not. They're her breasts. She can decide what size she wants them to be. But I decide it's best not to say anything and nod meekly. "Good, now step aside."

I move quickly as she pushes past me. When she's gone, I finally breathe out. Then I hear ... laughing? From inside the cupboard? Am I imagining it or is that the sound of the fates actually mocking me?

Joe comes crashing out from behind the beach ball collection. A few balls and a giant inflatable duck skid across the floor.

"Oh my god." Joe cannot stop laughing.

"Joe!" I whisper-shriek. "What are *you* doing in here?! What is it with this cupboard?!"

But Joe can't catch his breath. I don't think I've ever seen him like this.

"Oh my god... I'm sorry. But that was so funny." Eventually he stops laughing and carries on. "I come in here to get changed sometimes. When Belinda came in I hid because..." He stops. His gaze follows mine, which has slid down to his chest.

I am suddenly *very aware* that Joe is shirtless. And judging from the blush creeping up his neck, Joe is now *very aware* that Joe is shirtless.

I've never seen Joe shirtless. I don't think I ever imagined there was anything under Joe's shirt at all. He's just shirt, and trouser, and that's it. No skin. No, ahem, muscles.

Joe has *muscles?!?!*

SINCE WHEN?!

Joe sees me ogling his chest and covers himself with the inflatable duck. Oh great. Now my best mate thinks I'm a pervert. He's using a child's toy to cover himself from my pervy stare. I mean, ahem, my not-pervy stare. My regular stare. I'm not *perving*. I'm just surprised, that's all!!! Surprised that Joe has . . . skin.

"I get changed in here sometimes because, I don't know, yeah, all the other men, you know. I mean not that I'm *not* a man. I'm a man, they're men. Just, they're very . . . manly MEN. Do you know what I'm saying? I'm not embarrassed of my body or anything, sometimes it's just easier."

He's rambling again. I don't know how to respond. So in the end I say, "Don't be embarrassed. You've got skin."

Yes. Great. That makes everything much less awkward.

"Would you mind passing me my shirt? It's. . ." He points to the corner behind me.

"Oh sure, sure." I reach for the shirt and pass it to him, and turn around as he puts it on.

"OK, well, see you, M." He punches me on the shoulder as he leaves.

"Yeah, see you," I manage.

When he's gone it's finally just me in the cupboard. I

143

spend a good few minutes trying to dislodge the image of Joe's chest from my mind and prepare myself to go back out there. As a lifeguard. (I squash the slight twinge of guilt that I feel at having inadvertently duped my way into the role.) I've wanted to be a lifeguard since I got here. I can't count the number of times I've been scrubbing a toilet wishing I was outside sipping a smoothie. But I suddenly realize... When I'm cleaning I can basically be anywhere, mopping or dusting ... *hiding*. When I'm a lifeguard there's only one place I can be...

Right next to Aimee and Joe, on a tall chair, at the *very centre* of the pool.

How am I going to avoid all three boys, sitting *right in front of them?!*

CHAPTER

TWELVE

I step out of the cupboard feeling pretty smug. I've cracked it. The key to my invisibility, my disguise, my camouflage...

Flamingo sunglasses.

...And a sombrero.

There were loads hanging around in the cupboard for the big luau party. I just had to choose the most ridiculous items in there (flamingo-shaped sunglasses and giant sombrero) and hide behind them. I usually just wear casual leggings and tees, so no one would think it was me wearing anything so outlandish. And no one would think I'm a lifeguard because they think I'm the cleaner. So they'll just be all, "Hey, who's that new lifeguard with the wacky fashion sense?" and someone else will be all, "Dunno, man," and everyone will move on.

That is *exactly how this is going to go.*

I breathe and head towards the lifeguard chairs, where Aimee and Joe are already sitting. Joe has his shirt back on. Not that I'm still thinking about what's underneath it. I get a few looks as I walk along the pool, but they don't know who they're looking at, do they? I should say Mysterious Sombrero Girl gets a few looks as she walks down the pool. Should I experiment with a new walk too? *Yeah.* I think Mysterious Sombrero Girl would walk like a *boss.* I start dipping my shoulders heavily as I move and take confident steps towards Aimee and Joe.

"What. Are. You. Doing?" Aimee asks when I get there. Joe just has his mouth open.

"Sorry, who are you?" Mysterious Sombrero Girl asks. Damn, she has a husky voice.

"Oh my God," Aimee says. "It's finally happened. You've lost your mind. You've snapped!"

I lift up the flamingo sunglasses. "You can really tell it's me?"

"*Yes,*" laughs Aimee in disbelief. "Now climb up on this chair. Joe got you an extra one."

Just then Belinda pops up behind Aimee. "This arrangement is strictly for today *only,*" she says.

"Tomorrow we'll be back to two lifeguards on shift at a time. But *unfortunately* I can't send one of you home now, so." She looks wistful. Then she seems to notice what I'm wearing. "Maya, I appreciate you attempting to breathe a little life into your wardrobe, but now isn't the time. Please take off the dodo glasses and get to work."

Aimee bursts out laughing.

"*Fine*." I sigh and fling off the hat and "dodo glasses", then climb up on to my chair. I feel so *exposed*. Belinda passes by underneath me.

"And remember, *not a word*," she hisses behind her hand.

I don't know why she thinks I care so much about the contents of her bra. I'm sure her boobs look great with or without fillers. Anyway, what's underneath her clothes is really none of my business. But if it means I get to sit next to my two best friends in the crazy, unprecedented hot summer heat all day doing *absolutely nothing,* I won't contradict her.

"*Not a word*," I reply solemnly.

She nods and walks away.

It finally sinks in. I *am* sitting next to my two best friends. In the crazy, unprecedented hot summer heat. Doing absolutely nothing. (Provided no one starts to drown). I sit back and look at the pool glistening in the sunshine. Someone has set up a volleyball net over the water and two teams are punching the ball back and forth at each other. Drops of water spray over the players every time the ball hits the surface and everyone laughs.

I watch Belinda strutting around with her chest pushed out, "managing", and Belinda's friends stretched out on sunloungers lathering themselves up with oil. I look across at Aimee, who's closed her eyes and is bobbing along to the music from the café, and at Joe who's intently watching the swimmers in case he's needed. Suddenly I'm filled with a wild, untethered joy. No, this wasn't the summer I had planned. *It's better.*

"M, fetch us a drink, love." Aimee keeps her eyes closed but waves her hand in the direction of the bar.

"Ehm, no," I say. "Noah's over there."

I glance over at the tiki café, where I can see him standing in the shadows, staring into the mid distance. Only he could manage to look moody on a glorious day like today.

It's *highly attractive.*

"Oh, I figured you'd want to escape Adam and Jake," she says breezily.

"Escape... Wha...?" I look around to find what she means. In the distance I see Adam and Jake both heading this way, Jake from the right side of the pool and Adam from the left. *They're closing in*.

This would never have happened if I was allowed my brilliant disguise!!!

"How did you even see them?" Joe asks, looking at Aimee's closed eyes.

She opens one eye and winks at him. "I see everything, Joseph."

"All right, all right, I'm going!" I jump down from the chair and run to the café. On the way I run past Adam.

"Hey. . ." he starts.

"HEY, sorry, drinks run!" I reply, tapping my wrist and grimacing as if the drinks run is literally life or death. (Which, actually sometimes, if you meet Aimee on a sugar low, it is.) I leg it past him and approach the café.

By this point, I have realized I need a new plan. My disguise didn't work. *Fine*. Maybe avoiding all three boys all day long was highly unrealistic and unnecessary. Maybe the only thing I really need to do is avoid talking to them all *at the same time*. Much easier, right?

Right?

"Hey, Noah." I smile.

My words seem to pull him out of a deep, immersive daydream. What *is* he thinking about?

"Oh, hi," he smiles back.

I'm briefly under the spell of being in close proximity to Noah and his stare and his fringe again, when I remember I've got no time for that. *Pull yourself together, Burton. Stay alert.*

"Virgin colada smoothie for madam up there?" Noah gestures to Aimee.

"Hit the nail on the head," I say.

"What about you? What can I make you?" he asks.

"Oh, I don't know. What kind of other smoothies are there? Cuddles on the Beach?" I joke.

He smirks. "That is one, yeah. Coming up!"

Who knew? Noah launches into an impressive show of peeling, chopping, stirring, shaking. . . He even throws the bottle up in the air behind him and catches it on the back of his hand.

"Where did you learn to do that?" I gasp.

He just smiles knowingly. *So mysterious.*

Whilst he's making the drinks I make sure to keep checking behind me for any signs of Adam or Jake. Adam is back in the water and Jake has been stopped by some dog-lovers who are patting Stefan. I'm safe for now.

"So you had fun at the gig?" Noah asks, eyes still on his mocktails.

"Oh, so much fun." I glance behind me to check no one can hear.

"Good, me too." He looks up briefly, straight at me, with an expression I can't quite work out. Of course.

After Noah's done pouring and finishing with some bright, colourful umbrellas, he pushes three drinks across the counter at me. "And I made a watermelon cooler for Joe."

It's contained in an actual watermelon. I already know Joe's going to be pleased. Drinking out of a hollowed-out fruit is exactly the kind of novelty activity that excites him. Suddenly the picture of him drinking it, shirtless, comes into my head. I don't know why seeing him without his shirt on has disturbed me so much! I saw Aimee bending over in a thong from behind once and it didn't haunt me nearly as much... Probably because Joe was so uncomfortable and Aimee just laughed and said, "Do you like my thong, M?"

"That will be fifteen pounds," Noah says.

Fifteen pounds?! For three drinks? How is Aimee drinking so many of these? She must be in debt by now!

I pay and take the drinks, balancing mine awkwardly on the rim of Joe's watermelon. "Thank you, barkeep," I joke.

I breathe a sigh of relief as I turn away. One down, two to go. I'm sure that if I take control and greet them all individually before they can approach me, thus warding off any potential group interactions, then *everything will be fine*. They'll be none the wiser about my three eggs in three baskets. For all they know I'm just regular old, one-egg Maya.

The path ahead looks clear and boy-free. I start heading back to Aimee and Joe. Approximately twenty steps until I'm out of the "highly approachable" danger zone that walking alone leaves me in. I am moving as fast as humanly possible carrying multiple drinks... Eighteen... Fifteen... *Ten*... I've nearly made it to safety, when Adam springs out of the water like a beautiful, muscle-bound dolphin. He climbs out and stands in front of me, sweeping his wet hair off his face.

"Sook! I'd hug you but. . ." He gestures to the water dripping down his body. I try not to look. "How's it going? I see you got a promotion. How'd you swing that?"

I caught my boss amplifying parts of her anatomy using minimally toxic, highly heat-resistant ovals of synthetic compound.

"I guess Belinda finally spotted my life-saving potential," I say. Given that we met when I slipped and fell into a pool, I imagine that answer is not entirely convincing.

"Good deal. So if I fall in, is it your turn to rescue me?"

I laugh. My days, I'd forgotten the six pack... *Stay*

focused, Maya. I glance behind me at Noah, who is focused on wiping the counter, and at Jake who's still talking to the dog-lovers. It would have been better to find Adam later in a more private area, but maybe I can tick our chat off the list now. I might *just about* get away with it.

We keep talking, my stomach clenched the whole time. I'm barely listening to what Adam's saying and glancing between Noah and Jake. After a few minutes I'm about to head back with the drinks, thinking *yes, two done, one to go*! The chance of being approached by multiple boys at the same time is decreasing by the second. But then Stefan ruins *everything*.

Finally bored of being petted by random people, he spots me across the pool and starts barking. *Please don't come over here pleasedon'tcomeoverhere.*

Noooooooo!!! He's coming over here.

Stefan bounds towards me, barking louder and louder as he gets closer. Aghhhhhhhhh, why?! *Stupid adorable ball of useless life-ruining lovable fluff!!!*

MUST YOU HAVE SO MUCH LOVE INSIDE YOU?!

"Who's this little guy?" Adam bends down to the approaching dog.

I look to the other side of the pool and see Jake

153

following Stefan. He waves at me. "He's a stray. Quite a menace, actually," I say. "He bit me once. Don't touch him. Stay away!"

But Adam is already rubbing Stefan's head and Stefan is *lapping it up*. Predictable little attention-seeker.

"Aw, he seems all right. Hey, buddy." Adam keeps stroking him.

"Hi!" Jake nears us. I must look like a rabbit caught in headlights. I definitely feel like it. My heart is going a *million miles an hour*. "Sorry about him," he says to Adam. "He's a bit too friendly for his own good."

Fear. Anxiety. Fear.

"Oh, no problem, he's a good doggo." Adam finally stands up. "How old is he?"

Panic. Throat closing. Panic.

"About six months. He's trouble."

Just then Noah heads over to collect some empty glasses from the table right next to us. WHAT IS HAPPENING WHY IS THIS HAPPENING TO ME. Before he takes the glasses, he bends down to the dog too.

"Good boy," he whispers. How does everything he says make him sound like he's doing the voiceover for a luxury chocolate advert?!

Horror. Alarm. Horror.

Jake turns to me. "You all right, Maya?"

"Fine," I croak. I clear my throat. "But I've got to get this drink to Aimee before she dies of thirst. She's been working so hard, poor girl."

Just at that moment we all look over at Aimee who pulls Joe's cap over his eyes, laughs for a bit, then leans back and stifles a big yawn.

Dammit, Aimee!!!

"Anyway, best be off." I try to style it out. "See ya."

My heart is still racing as I walk away, and I feel like I might pass out. I'm just starting to think *I did it, I did it, I did it,* when Jake yells, "No problem. Want to take Stefan for another walk later? We'll go out for dinner this time."

Even though it's thirty degrees out, I swear the air turns frosty. My blood runs so cold it's like ice is filling my veins. I feel three pairs of eyes boring into my back. *Is there any chance the other two didn't hear that...?!*

I turn back to look at them. Adam has one eyebrow raised and Noah's brows are knitted together. Jake's noticed their reaction and his eyes dart between them.

Nope. Not a chance.

THIRTEEN

"I can't *believe* you made it out of that alive." Aimee cackles. "You get uncomfortable choosing whether to greet someone with an air kiss or a hug."

"You know, for someone who got me into this mess in the first place, you're not incredibly supportive," I huff.

It's later that evening and we're all at my house. My breathing rate his finally returned to normal. It took me all day, and a copious number of Jaffa cakes, to calm down. For someone who lives in constant fear of even slightly awkward social situations, (seriously, what if you go for an air kiss *at the same time* as they go for a hug?!), today was essentially my idea of a living hell.

Once Jake had spoken, I could tell they were all trying to piece the situation together in their minds. After they had finished looking between each other and then at me, it became clear I was the one who was supposed to fill the silence with some random selection of words. *Yet again,* I considered jumping in the pool. There was a slight chance that if I did die all three of them would still say nice things about me at my funeral. Not "RIP Maya, she was a snakey sort with too many eggs."

I took one last-ditch attempt at making a choice between the three of them, by listening out for any loud breathers. I checked carefully they were all taking air in and out... Nope, all nice and quiet. *Damn.*

"So, um." I cleared my throat. "Yeah. I went on a date with each of you."

I could barely get the words out because my mouth was so parched. I'd never wished so hard for anything as I wished for the power of invisibility at that moment. They said nothing, so I searched my head for more words. *Any words.* What was that thing Aimee said that made it sound way less snakey than it felt? "I just wanted to *get to know* each of you?" I finally added.

I held my breath, preparing myself for the inevitable fallout. The hurt eyes, the arms thrown in the air, the shouts of "How could you?!" I was genuinely wincing. Were they going to start hissing and shouting "snake" and pelting me with rotten fruit?!

Noah spoke first. "That's really OK, Maya..." The way he said it I had *absolutely no clue* whether he meant it or not. But then, what's new? He looked like he was about to add something else, but then Adam interrupted.

"Yeah, sook, no worries," Adam said. "It's early days."

"Don't worry, Maya. It is what it is." Jake shrugged.

It's *early days?!?!*

It is what it is?!

That was *not* the response I was expecting. Pure relief flooded my entire body. My icy blood returned to a normal temperature. My shoulders, which were clenched up to my neck, dropped down. *Oh my days. Thank goodness.*

After that, Noah pretty much headed back to work, Adam dived back into the pool and Jake took Stefan off to stretch his legs. I stood blinking in the sunlight, unable to compute what had just happened.

"So you're just ... casually being grafted by three boys? Who all found out about each other and are fine with it?" Aimee whistles. "Ooh, poor Maya, she has *such problems*. However will she choose between all these sexy boys running around after her?"

"Someone's not bitter at all," adds Joe.

Aimee laughs. "No, honestly, M, I'm pleased for you.

You need a bit of a confidence boost after slumming it with Empty Box for so long. Just don't complain to the rest of us mere mortals about having too many love interests, please. Some of us are having a *dry* summer." She gestures to Joe and herself.

"Thanks, Aimee," Joe says flatly.

"Well, I guess it's not just the summer for you, is it?" she says. "A dry . . . year?"

"Hey!" Joe whines. "There was that . . . girl."

"Imaginary girl?" Aimee raises her eyebrows.

"She was real," Joe mutters.

"I'm only going to say this once, Joe, girls in video games aren't real."

"The girl from Starbucks," Joe responds, awkwardly yet stubbornly. "You know, the big cup mix-up?"

"OH MY GOD! *Her!*" Aimee shrieks. "Oh my God, Joe and Jo getting each other's cups. The best meet-cute *ever*. How could I forget?! What happened there?"

"I didn't see it going anywhere." Joe glances at me awkwardly. He probably feels guilty about telling Aimee and not me.

Joe dated a girl? An actual, *real-life girl?!* Why didn't Joe tell *me*? What else do Joe and Aimee know about each other that I don't? This whole conversation is making me feel funny. Or was I feeling funny anyway, from the three-boys-who-are-apparently-fine-with-there-being-three-boys situation? Maybe I have sunstroke.

"Is that what happened?" Aimee jokes. "Or did she hear how you've never been last one standing in *Fortnite* and run a mile?"

"All right, too far, Ames. You're gonna *pay*." Joe dives on her and she puts her hands up like claws. They roll around for a bit whilst Joe tickles her and Aimee squeals. All right ... *get a room*. Not for the first time I wonder if Aimee and Joe are going to get together one day. Now I *definitely* feel funny ... like, nauseous funny. I have so much fear about what would happen if they did start dating, because it might mess up our friendship group.

Eventually I bring them back to the matter at hand. "Ehm," I say. "This rough and tumble is making me *highly uncomfortable*. You're destroying my neatly organized bedroom."

They stop. "Sorry, M," Joe apologises.

I feel my guts settle as they stop tickling each other. I was feeling genuinely sick.

"Yeah, so." Aimee settles back down on the bed. "What's the plan of action?"

"Well, I'm glad you asked that, Aimee." I open my drawer and get out the pro/con list I made. It's colour-coordinated (red for serious considerations, yellow for medium, green for minor) as well as being cross-referenced (some of the boys may have the same considerations going for them) and each guy is scored using a point system. "I thought if I wrote everything down in an ordered way, like when I'm trying to work out a chemistry problem, it might help."

"And did it?" Aimee asks.

I clutch it against my chest protectively because I know Aimee will mock it, but eventually I hand it to her. She gawps at it. Joe looks over her shoulder.

"As you can see, I've written each of their totals at the bottom there." I point.

"Each of these totals is exactly the same," Joe states.

"*I know that, Joe! That's the problem!*" I yelp. "So, my POA is clear: I must find out at least *one thing* about each guy that takes them up or down by the end of the week."

"M, we've been down this route before," Aimee says evenly. "We did the pros and cons thing earlier. Adding a few colour categories into the mix isn't going to help. Come on, you must have a gut feeling. Close your eyes..." She takes on a deep, soothing voice. "Which one do you seeeeee."

I close my eyes. "Urmm, I see Adam's arms... Oh wait, no, there are Noah's eyes, and Jake's smile." OMD. My head has been turned so many times I can't even look in one direction for a second any more. My head is *spinning!!!*

"I give up, M." Aimee shrugs. "But the good thing is now you have permission to date them all at once, so, just relax and enjoy it."

She picks up the list and throws it to one side nonchalantly using one hand, scrolling through her phone in the other. Joe stoops over to pick it up for me and folds it up on my table. He gives me a small smile as he lays it down.

"Uhhh ... M?" Aimee says. Her tone is properly weird. Like in a horror movie when one character has just spotted a ghost hovering behind another person's head holding an axe.

"What?"

She's looking at her phone. She holds it up for me and Joe to see. It's a photo of Lydia. At first glance I think she's in Spain – she's in her bikini, looking annoyingly tanned and glossy – but then I see the telltale sign of "Casa Nadar" behind her head.

She's *here?!* Why isn't she in Spain?

Does that mean Freddie's here too?!

I take a closer look at her post. It says: *Back from Europe to a surprise Indian Summer...* My heart pounds in my chest. Freddie had been so out of sight, out of

162

mind, almost like he stopped being real. But the thought he might now be back in the same country hits me like a bucket of freezing cold water. It makes him feel more real than ever and everything else that's happened this summer morphs into a hazy, distant dream.

"Why are they back early?" Joe frowns.

Aimee doesn't say anything, just flicks on to Lydia's next post with one eyebrow raised. It's a picture of Lydia and Jake. I repeat: *a picture of Lydia and Jake!*

Suddenly everything clicks into place. That comment Belinda made when I was round Jake's house, about him being back in town to see someone. I'd kind of forgotten about it, to be honest. I'd been so distracted by nearly burning down his kitchen and by everything that was going on. Is it possible that she meant Lydia?

In the picture Jake has his arm around her. They're both in their swimwear at Casa Nadar. They must have arrived just a few hours after our shift ended, because I didn't see her. The caption reads: *Been so long since I've seen my fave boy #reunion #whosaysexescantbefriends. . .*

Who says exes *can't be friends?!*

Exes?!

OMD. Is this *for real?*

"Jake went out with Lydia?" I ask quietly, even though the answer is obvious. "Oh my days. I feel like such an idiot."

Jake was never here to dog-sit. He was here to see ex-girlfriend Lydia! He must have been massively disappointed when he realized she was living it up in Spain instead. Suddenly all the familiar feelings of rejection that I had when Freddie took Lydia to Spain instead of me start creeping back in. I feel like a massive consolation prize.

"I just messaged Amanda from art class and *she* says Jake and Lydia went out nearly a year ago, and Lydia dumped him. Funny how she's come back all the way from Spain, now that *you're* seeing Jake," Aimee practically growls.

"No." I shake my head. "How would Lydia have even known about me and Jake? I definitely didn't post any pictures of us."

Aimee flicks on to Jake's Instagram and clicks on a picture of Stefan running through the park, from when we took him for a walk, with the caption "#thirdwheelingdog #romanticstroll". "You're tagged in this."

"Oh," I say, studying the picture. I hadn't been on Instagram in a couple of days. I guess I was enjoying the peace and quiet of not seeing Freddie and Lydia's constant updates. "OK, so, she might have found out, but why would she come all the way back from Spain for that?"

"Because she's jealous," Aimee mutters darkly.

"Why would she be *jealous?!* They're not going out any more, and she was in *Spain!* Who could be jealous of anyone else when they were lying on a beach in Spain?"

"People like that always want what they can't have," Aimee states matter-of-factly. "A holiday was more interesting than Jake when she was taking it from you. Now someone else wants Jake and he's all shiny again."

"No, Lydia's nice," I defend. I think back to the message she sent to check I was all right about her going with Freddie. OK, granted, it didn't make me feel any better, but I had believed it was sent with the best of intentions.

"She's a princess, M."

I look at the photo of them again. They do look very . . . *cosy*.

"Well, I can't exactly complain, can I? I mean, I was the one who asked to just *see where things go*. It would be pretty rotten of me to be jealous now."

Except I *obviously am*.

"Well, I think we've found something for your list, M." Aimee grabs a pen and unfolds the list from where Joe left it on the table. Joe and I peer over her shoulder as she writes "dated Lydia McKenzie" in Jake's column, scribbles out his score and changes it to minus one hundred.

CHAPTER

FOURTEEN

The next morning at the pool, it's just Joe and me on lifeguard duty until Aimee arrives for the afternoon shift. Joe and I are sitting having a ferocious thumb war, when I see Lydia appear at the far end of the pool. She's wearing a white bikini which contrasts beautifully against her golden skin and her hair is pulled back into a long, swishy ponytail that swings from side to side as she struts down the walkway. (I never understand girls that have ponytails with no flyaway hairs. Why do my ponytails always leave me with a halo of fuzz that makes me look like I've been electrocuted?)

My heart starts beating double time. I'm not quite sure why. It's not like Lydia and I technically have any beef. But the fact she's just been on holiday with my ex-boyfriend and I've just had a date with hers doesn't make for the *most natural* of social situations.

She waves at the group of girls who have been dominating the "beach area" all summer and goes to sit with them. Together they look like an ad campaign for some sort of fashion brand's swimwear range.

"How do they get their bodies to look like that?" I ask Joe, distracted from our thumb war. He was winning anyway.

"Like what?" He looks at them.

"...Toned."

I realize mine and Joe's hands are still touching and pull away.

"They go to the gym more than once a year," answers Joe. "And they don't eat so many Jaffa cakes."

Joe is referring to the time I went to the school gym and left after ten minutes because it was much harder work than sitting on my sofa. It occurs to me that Joe must go the gym, too, given ... um, what his body looks like. Who knew? *No. Don'thinkaboutthatdon'tthink aboutthatdon'thinkaboutthat. He is your friend. There is nothing under Joe's shirt.*

"Maybe I should try again," I suggest. But as soon as I say it I know in my heart it is never going to happen. "But I really like Jaffa cakes and lying down."

"Nah. You're perfect just as you are."

It's strange. If Aimee had said something similar I wouldn't have blinked. But when Joe says it, I feel very aware of myself. Suddenly I can feel my hands and feet and the sun on my skin and the bead of sweat running down my back. Joe must feel awkward too because he embarks on a classic Joe ramble.

"I mean..." He clears his throat. "I guess perfect depends on your definition of perfection. What *is* perfection? There's so much pressure on body image and *living your best life* and, maybe you can like your body toned and your best life can be constantly taking your rock-hard muscles travelling and climbing mountains, or going gigging around Europe, or saving tiny adorable animals from perilous situations but ... I don't know ... maybe you can like your body full of Jaffa cakes, and maybe sometimes your best life can be just sitting down and watching some really crap TV after doing your homework." He takes a big breath.

I don't have time to respond to any of this, because I'm distracted by Lydia getting up from her sunlounger and starting a purposeful walk in my direction. She looks straight at me as her hips sway gracefully from side to side. How does she manage to be so light-footed in those giant heels?!

As she approaches us she ignores Joe and pats me lightly on the arm. Which apparently she can reach, even though I am higher up than her on the lifeguard chair, because she is about a hundred feet tall.

"Hi, babe?" She smiles at me, barely tilting her head up. "Can I pull you for a quick chat?"

"Oh, er. . ." My throat, which was already dry from the heat, dehydrates like the Sahara desert. *Pull me for a chat? What's this about?!* "Sure," I say finally.

I climb down from my chair. She flashes me another beam and turns on her heel. I guess I'm expected to go after her. I turn back to Joe and we shrug at each other before I follow.

She gets to a pair of vacant sunloungers and sits down, crossing her legs and patting the space beside her. I dutifully sit down.

I wait for her to speak but she doesn't. So even though she was the one who asked to talk to me, my need to avoid *any hint of awkwardness whatsoever* takes over. "How was your holiday?" I ask.

As soon as I say it I think of her and Freddie lying in the sun, Freddie not having a second thought for me, and I want to cry. I've not wanted to cry in weeks. I can hear Aimee in my head going, "Why did you ask her how her holiday was?! You don't want to hear about that! You overly polite British fool! SELF-CARE, MAYA!"

Thankfully Lydia's answer isn't expansive. "Good, thanks," she says.

I hate myself for it, but I want to know if Freddie's still out there or not. "Why did you come back early?" I ask, *hopefully subtly*.

"Freddie's still out there," she says.

Of course. Lydia's a girl-girl. She can sniff out *a mile off* when someone is fishing for information about their ex. I feel a blush creeping up my neck. But I'm glad I did fish, because now I don't have to panic about Freddie turning up.

"... just *so* boring." I'm so relieved about the geographical distance between Freddie and me, I've forgotten Lydia is still talking. "Why stay in Spain if it's raining there and thirty degrees at home?"

I mean, I can think of a few reasons... To spend time with her friend. To not be rude to the people who flew her out there. But maybe I worry too much about everything.

"So, I just wanted to talk to you about this Jake thing?" she continues.

"Oh," I say. I wasn't expecting that. I'm not sure what I was expecting. "OK..."

"So obviously it was a shock to see Jake posting about

you. I messaged Belinda and when she confirmed you went out with him. I was just a bit surprised that you'd done it before talking to me? Given our history?"

Belinda! Suddenly it all falls into place. Of course she's friends with Belinda. . . Lydia is on the football team and Belinda was her captain! I try to process all this new information. *What?!* What is she accusing me of? But . . . I didn't even know he was Lydia's ex! And even if I had known . . . didn't Aimee say they went out a year ago and she broke up with him? Before I have a chance to defend myself she carries on.

"You know like how I checked it was all right with you before I went away with Freddie? *Girl code?*"

She didn't *technically* check with me before doing it. She just sent me a message saying she "hoped it wasn't awkward". And the thought occurs to me that even if she had asked my permission to go with Freddie, would I really have been able to say anything about it? "No, please don't take up the opportunity of an exciting holiday in Europe and stay here in the UK instead, because otherwise I will be insanely jealous." And if I had dared to say that, would she have stayed? We're not even that good friends. . .

"Obviously if you had talked to me I would have been fine with it?" Lydia goes on. "It was just a blow for me because I'm quite a loyal person? Anyway, I really don't want to fight, I wanted to talk to you because Jake and I have been speaking, and what we have is very *real* and there are still feelings there. We want to get back together but I wanted to talk to you first?"

My head is spinning. And not in the good, too-many-hot-boys kind of way, in the I-don't-know-what-is-happening kind of way. She's finally stopped talking and seems to expect me to say something. I have *no idea* how to reply.

"I mean, of course, obviously," I say. "If you both want to get back together then of course you should."

"Oh, amazing, I'm *so* glad we had this chat, babe. So good to clear the air and obviously I wouldn't want us to not be OK? Have a good day, yeah, and I'll catch you around?" She air-kisses me and walks off before I can reply.

I feel confused and jumbled and like there were a million things I wanted to say and didn't. But mostly I just feel *awful*. I felt bad enough about dating three guys on its own, let alone without other girls getting sucked into it… I can't believe my thinly spread eggs have caused so much chaos! I'm just a snake! A big, poisonous old snake!!! I would never want to get in the way of what Lydia and Jake have, if it's that real.

At that moment a message from Jake pops up on my phone. I see his name and delete it before I can even read it. I don't need another pity rejection message like the one I got from Freddie. It's "cool, cool, cool" as Aimee would say. He wants to be with Lydia. They have a "history". I completely get it. I was surprised he was even interested in me in the first place, so this makes perfect sense.

I head back over to Joe and climb up my chair. He peers at me. "Hey, everything all right?"

"I think so," I say quietly.

Joe obviously senses everything is *not* all right. He hesitantly puts a hand on my shoulder. "Did the inflection of her voice rise at the end of every sentence like a que*stion?* Even when she's not really asking a que*stion?*"

His impression of Lydia is so spot on that, even though I am feeling like the lowliest snake girl ever to slither through the swamps of love, I have to laugh.

And then, just when I think this day can't get any worse, Adam appears. Ordinarily that would make my day *better*, but I can tell as soon as I see him that something isn't right. Usually the expression on his face makes you want to start singing "Hakuna Matata". But he has a single frown line creasing his perfectly smooth, worry-free forehead. And he's heading straight for me.

"Sook, can I grab you for a chat?"

What is it with everyone wanting a "chat" today?! No!!! No you can't have a bloody chat! No more!! *The snake is tired!!! SNAKES NEED REST TOO.*

Obviously I don't say that. I get up and follow him.

"Maya," he says. He just used my real name. This must be serious. He doesn't have a secret ex-girlfriend in my social circle, does he?! I swear, if he snogged Belinda. . .

"There's no easy way to say this, but I'm going to be cutting my trip short. Well, this part of the trip." He shoves his hands in his short pockets. "I've been discovered."

I blink. This is the second conversation of the day to not go at all how I was expecting.

". . .Discovered?" I repeat.

"A model scout wants to sign me up to their agency. They want me to be part of a new travel campaign they're doing in partnership with a big fashion brand."

I blink again. "What does that mean?"

"It means I can finally travel around the world, unhampered by monetary considerations, unimpeded by material possessions."

"You mean . . . someone is giving you a free holiday and dressing you?"

He laughs. "Going to miss your way with words, sook."

It dawns on me that Adam's actually leaving. I always knew he was leaving at some point, but I thought we had the rest of the summer to, as Aimee put it, "see where things went". I guess not. I feel a bit numb and deflated. At least I don't think I'm going to burst into tears on the spot. That will probably come later . . . once I'm alone in my bedroom and have properly digested the news.

"I'm going to miss you too . . . but that's amazing!" I try to sound sincere. It *is* a great opportunity for him. "Well done!"

"Cheers, as you poms will say." Adam shoots me his classic crooked smile. "My flight's this evening, so. . ."

"So soon?!" I'm desperately trying not to sound too tragic. The tan!! The muscles!!! I didn't even get to see them one last time. He could have *at least* taken his shirt off to say goodbye!

"Bye, sook." He cups my chin in his big, firm hands. I think about saying we could see each other when he gets back but then don't. After all, I'm the one who wanted to "keep my options open". It would be a bit rich for me to ask him to wait for me now, wouldn't it? Plus, my lips are squished between his fingers, like a puffer fish. (I don't think he realizes his own strength.) With one last, remorseful sigh, Adam turns to go.

As he walks, the thud of his footsteps make drinks ripple in their glasses. He really is quite big.

I trudge back over to Joe, who is pulling a grimace. "That didn't look good," he says.

"It wasn't," I reply. "He's gone."

Joe opens his mouth, closes it again, then opens it again. "I almost don't want to show you this, but..." He pulls up his phone and hands it to me. I reach for it reluctantly. What is it now? What else could *possibly happen today?!*

On Joe's screen is a video of Noah. He's aggressively strumming his guitar and singing. Joe turns on the volume.

> *"Proper melt;*
> *Never wanted to become one;*
> *Proper melt;*
> *Not for the wrong someone;*
> *Proper melt, proper melt, proper melt;*
> *Now it's time to let go;*
> *Proper melt, proper melt, proper melt;*
> *Can't stick around for this, no;*
> *Proper melt..."*

Underneath the video is a caption: "This song is called 'Proper Melt', and it's about being done waiting around for a girl who just isn't into me." I switch the phone off.

"ARGHHHHHHHHHHHHH!" I yell. "OH MY DAYS!" I bury my head in my hands. Joe pats me tentatively.

I never should have listened to Aimee. Not that this is anyone else's fault but my own. I should have put all my eggs in *one basket* from the beginning. Then maybe I wouldn't have any of these problems, or I'd be able to do something about them! But I have got eggs in baskets all over the place and they are *all smashed!!!!*

I'VE DROPPED ALL MY EGGS!

I can't believe yesterday I was actually complaining about having *three guys* to swoon away the summer with... and now I have a big fat zero!

I really want to go home and wallow, maybe sport the indoor-sunglasses look again and have a good cry, but I don't need Belinda baying for my blood on top of everything else, so I stay put.

An hour later, Jake arrives at the pool. Lydia jumps up and starts waving, and he begins heading over to her. As he walks he waves in my direction. I give the smallest, least noticeable wave possible. It's practically a twitch. He looks a bit sad (probably the memory of having gone out with me when he was super in love with Lydia the whole time, and me burning down his kitchen for nothing) and goes and sits next to Lydia and her friends.

Do they have to make *such* an attractive couple?!

Noah turns up for his café shift and properly blanks me, like the Big Invisible Snake that I am. And the new swim teacher who shows up to take Adam's place is an old, middle-aged hairy man, which really rubs salt in the wound of his absence.

"Maya, you should probably stop staring." Joe's voice penetrates my cloud of hot boy-less doom.

"Was I staring?" I ask.

"Your eyes keep wandering between Noah, Jake and the hairy old dude taking Adam's class."

"If I squint *reeaally hard*, he could almost be Adam . . . wearing a fuzzy sweater." As I lean my head to one side, I finally realize how deranged I sound. When Joe suggests a game to take my mind off things, I quickly agree.

We spend the next three hours doing stupid things like playing "snog, marry, avoid" about all the people around the pool, offering to put sun cream on for someone just as their partner is about to do it, or daring each other to ask pool-goers strange questions with a totally serious face, like, "Sir, where *did* you buy your rather fetching Speedos?" (One man speaks in a totally serious, deadpan way about the manufacture of his Speedos for nearly twenty minutes.) My favourite is when Joe asks some parents if their kid's inflatable rubber duck is for sale, and they say no, so Joe offers them five-hundred pounds and you can tell they're thinking about it, even though the kid is gripping the duck tightly with large, fearful eyes.

I'm *nearly distracted* from my loss of eggs. Nearly.

When it's time to go home I have to walk past the café and the beach area to collect my things from the locker room. Noah is shaking up a smoothie for a group of girls and cleverly turns away as I walk past, as if it's part of the routine. Jake is too focused on Lydia and her friends to notice me. They're playing a game in which one person passes a post-it to another person using just their mouth, and if they drop it they have to kiss. Naturally, just as Lydia passes it to Jake she drops it on the floor and launches herself forward for a big, passionate snog.

I turn away because it hurts. Not that I'm justified in feeling hurt at all. If Jake's happy then I want to be happy for him. I suppose it just makes me feel that I'm never *not* going to be second best to shiny, self-assured people like Lydia.

Instead, I focus on dissing this game that I have never seen or heard of before. Because it is clearly not a *real game*, but a moronic excuse concocted by this group of randy teenagers to snog the person they fancy. (Not that I'm bitter.)

"Honestly, that is *so* immature," I say to Joe. "We're not twelve any more."

"Really?" Joe says. "I think it looks kind of fu—"

"Let me stop you right there, Joe. *Obviously* it's genius. *Obviously* I wish I could kiss the person I fancy with all peril of rejection removed, under the pretence it was "because the game made me". But can you play along for a second?! I need to vent."

Joe nods. "So immature," he agrees.

"Thank you." I nod, feeling reassured.

After what feels like a very, *very* long day, we exit the pool. Hairy Not Adam waves at us and bids us a good evening, and I want to throw myself in front of a car.

Joe and I walk along the road quietly until we get to the fork that takes us home in different directions. "Hey, M," he says. "I know you're upset. But earlier for a while you seemed like you were having fun. I mean, *I* was having fun at least. I don't know, are you sure you want to go home? We could go to mine. I mean ... it's not as exciting as climbing giant walls or going to secret gigs in converted churches, and I don't have a dog. My game collection isn't as impressive as your dad's, but I think we have a few in the loft and I've got a pizza. I don't know, yeah, just . . . if you feel like it."

I don't know why this invitation feels so strange. It shouldn't. Joe and I hang out *all the time*. But mainly when Aimee is there and usually at her house or mine. We don't go round to Joe's much. Aimee does sometimes, but I've never spent time there alone.

"Yeah, of course." I smile. I really do want to go round to Joe's. On second thought, it sounds much better than going home and wallowing in my sunglasses in my bedroom. As appealing as a good wallow can be. We set off together in the direction of Joe's house.

Just then we see Aimee running along the road towards us. "How late . . . am I?!" she pants.

I look at my phone. "Ten minutes."

"Crap! Belinda said . . . she would . . . wear my skin . . . if I was late again." Aimee bends over, breathing deeply. She stands up, as if to start running again, then stops. "Hang on. . . Where are you two going?"

"Joe's house," I say.

"Ah," she replies. I can't quite work out the tone in her voice. I thought she'd be more openly, jokingly annoyed we were going to hang out just as she was beginning her shift. I thought she might say something like, "All right, don't spare me a thought whilst I slave away, will you?" But there's something else in her voice instead. I try to work out what it is, but then catch sight of Jake meandering away from the pool area like he might leave, and pull on Joe's arm to hurry him up.

"You two kids have fun," she calls after us. "I'll see you tomorrow, hopefully. But if I don't show up then please point the police in Belinda's direction."

We wave her off and walk down the street, trying to play thumb wars and laughing about the man from earlier and his intricate knowledge of Speedo manufacture. En route I get multiple messages from Aimee.

> **Oh my God can Lydia please get a room for herself. Sorry you had to watch her fling herself at Jake all day!**
>
> **Gosh, Noah really IS moody! I asked him for my usual (virgin colada smoothie) and he was SUCH A PRINCESS about it.**
> **(Calling him a princess didn't help.)**
>
> **Is it just me or has Adam aged about thirty years since we last saw him? Ha-ha!**

Bless her trying to cheer me up.

We get to Joe's house and walk up the front pathway. As he lets us in I realize it's been a while since I've been to his place. Inside, the sound of daytime quiz-show music blares out. We wave to his gran, who's sitting on the sofa shouting answers at the TV.

"Oh hello, loves," she calls, turning in her armchair.

"Hi, Gran." Joe goes in and kisses her on the cheek.

"Hi, Mrs D!" I wave from the doorway.

"Hello, Maya!" she calls out. "It's good to see you. You're looking gooorgeous. Promise me you'll show off those legs whilst you've still got the chance, eh?"

I laugh. "I solemnly swear."

Joe blushes and says, "We're just going upstairs. Where are the twins?"

"In their room watching some sort of godawful movie about bald yellow creatures who run around in packs making godawful noises. They shouldn't bother you."

Joe nods and backs out of the room. We move to the kitchen to get a drink.

"Ehm!" She calls after us. "Keep the door open!"

Joe blushes. "Sorry," he mutters. "She was born in the forties. She still doesn't really believe men and women can be friends."

I smile. "It's all right. You should have seen my dad

the other day when Noah, Adam and Jake all showed up outside our house."

Joe clears his throat. "Yeah." He doesn't say anything else.

Joe pours me some squash and grabs a box of Jaffa cakes (he knows me so well). On the way upstairs it occurs to me, for the first time, what a female household Joe lives in. A gran, two mums and two sisters. No wonder his two best friends are women. I forgot how much I liked it here the last time I came round with Aimee. It feels full of life and ... girlish giggles. Upstairs you can still hear his gran's show blaring in the living room and his sisters squealing with laughter in their bedroom. I'm guessing his mums are out at work.

When we get to his room, we leave the door ajar. I look around Joe's room. It's minimal. And tidy (unlike Aimee's room). I assume it must be tidy all the time because he didn't even know I was coming round. His various game consoles are set up in front of a big TV. He has a few plants that, unlike me, he has successfully managed to keep alive. I suddenly feel ever so slightly uneasy. *I'm in Joe's bedroom.* But I brush it off. Of course I'm in Joe's bedroom, *he's my friend.*

There's a big poster of a snail on his wall.

"Who's that again?" I ask. I feel sure Joe's explained this before.

"It's Brian from the Magic Roundabout. He was my favourite," Joe says.

"Oh yeah. Why?" I ask.

Joe looks thoughtful. "I always remember that episode where he tried to race a train."

"Did he win?"

"No, he fell asleep on the way. But he tried." Joe shrugs.

Joe has an interesting way of looking at the world. I still sometimes can't believe that Aimee and I never used to notice him in class that much, because he's quiet. But now I realize that he may not be the loudest guy, but whatever he *does* say is unexpected and makes me think twice. Now I need Joe's opinion on everything. Who'd have thought?

"Want to play a game?" He gestures to his collection. "Aimee always smashes me so it would make a change to beat someone for once."

"You're so sure you're going to beat me?"

"I have to make up for Operation somehow."

I laugh. We go to sit on the beanbags in front of the TV. It's *very comfortable*. I can see why Joe hardly ever wants to leave his room. Behind the TV I notice some weights. So Joe does work out...

"Hardcore, having these in your room," I comment. "Don't get enough time in at the gym?" I reach forward and grab one. I pretend to lift it as a joke but my arm ends up buckling under it.

"Ha *ha*. You sound like Aimee." Joe pushes the weight back behind the TV. "I don't go to the gym any more. Don't like everyone watching me."

"What, all the other big, burly men comparing their biceps?" I tease.

"No ... the, uh." He coughs. "There's this group of girls in the year below that ... well. They keep looking at me and. . ." He makes his voice very quiet. "*Giggling.*"

When he says it I'm taking a sip of my squash and I almost spit it everywhere. I start choking. Joe leaps out of his beanbag and starts patting me on the back.

"You OK?" he asks when I've eventually stopped gasping for air.

I nod and play along like it was just a random gone-down-the-wrong-way situation. But honestly I was caught off guard by Joe having a Year Below Fan Club. We've all seen those girls. We've all *been* those girls. Staring at a gorgeous older boy across the room and group daydreaming about what they might be like. Me and Aimee had one (who knows what his name was) but he left a couple of years ago. Aimee called him FUOB. (Fit

Unattainable Older Boy. Pronounced "Fwob".) He ate a lot of apples. We used to watch him eating them. Ah, FUOB...

Joe is someone's FUOB?!

I guess I shouldn't be so surprised. I have seen him shirtless. *No!!! Don't think of Joe shirtless!* It took days to get that image out of my head and *now it's BACK!*

I blink the image away. Then I realize Joe's hand is still on my shoulder. I glance at it and he swiftly removes it, springing to one side. He coughs and yanks opens a drawer full of video games.

"All right, let's play Mario Kart," he says.

"Will I like it?" I ask.

Famous last words. Four hours later we're still playing. I've mainly lost but I've won a few times and every time I shout *very loudly.* I never thought I could get so excited over a short mushroom-hatted man driving a tiny pink car around a race track. But *damn I want to win!*

"Aha, take *that,* foolish ghost!" I say as I whiz around a corner.

"I'm going to knock that mushroom right off your head!" shouts Joe.

I'm brought out of my Mario Kart haze by a text from Dad.

You home tonight? Dad x

Whoops, it's nearly nine! Has it really been that long? Where did the time go?! It feels like ages ago I was watching Adam's retreating back as he flew off to his glamorous new life, Noah ignoring me as he made impressive drinks for ravening hordes of fangirls, and Lydia sucking post-its off Jake's face.

It's OK I'm at Joe's. Coming home x

Oh fine. Stay out as late as you want! Dad x

Dad loves Joe, almost as much as he loves Aimee. I'm sure if I said, "Oh, I'm just piloting a jet plane with Joe," or, "Oh, I'm just bungee jumping off a cliff with Joe," he'd say it was fine. But I should go home anyway. I've not spent much time with Dad this week. It would be nice to see him before he goes to bed.

Joe looks at the time and seems to read my mind. "You going home?" he asks.

I nod.

"I'll walk with you." He climbs out of his beanbag. "I go for a swim around this time anyway."

Joe *swims?!* Who *is* this person, who works out in his

room and goes for late night dips in the pool? How did I not know this? Come to think of it, I've learned quite a lot about Joe over the last couple of weeks that I had no idea about. That he goes to the gym, and the assault course, and listens to intense emotional music, and cooks...

"I see you looking surprised." He laughs. "It's a good time to go. Clears your head. Plus – no giggling girls."

I laugh, feeling slightly weird remembering that girls giggle over Joe. He reaches for my (good) hand and pulls me out of the beanbag, and as our hands touch, I suddenly feel very aware of my fingers. And Joe's fingers. Almost like I'm touching a stranger. I pull away quickly and shake myself. Obviously it's fine, our hands have been touching all day playing thumb wars... I think I've just psyched myself out thinking about Joe's fan club. They'd probably kill to touch Joe's hand.

We leave the house and walk through the dusky streets. The sun is nearly set but the air is still balmy. I inhale the air deeply and take in the smell of honeysuckle. Is the summer here always this wonderful? Why had I never noticed before? I look beside me at Joe, who is staring up at the fading purple sky. Why was I so desperate to spend the holidays in Spain when all this was on my doorstep?

I say goodbye to Joe at the pool and carry on home.

I realize that, even though I wasn't in a different, exotic country or trying an extreme sport or doing anything particularly exciting at all, the whole night has flown by and I've not thought about Adam, Noah, Jake, Lydia, Freddie or even Belinda once.

CHAPTER

FIFTEEN

The next day, for the first time since I got the "it's over" message from Freddie, I wake up with a sense of calm. Freddie is still a million miles away (OK, for the sake of geographical accuracy I should point out he's actually a thousand miles away, but a million sounds far more dramatic) which makes me feel peaceful. And yes, so yesterday I got dumped by three amazing guys... But dating three amazing guys was the most stressful experience of my *entire life*.

Obviously I'm slightly disappointed my summer romance(s) were cut short. *Obviously* I will build a shrine to Adam's muscles and Noah's hair and Jake's eyes and pray to it every night. *Obviously* I will always be baffled that the same spooky, universal forces that saw fit to bring

Hot Dog, Hot Sauce and Hot Plate into my life also saw fit to snatch them away. But, even though I know Aimee would be gravely disappointed in me for thinking this. . .

HURRAH FOR BEING DUMPED!

The sun is shining. Birds are singing. Children are playing. I am free, free, *freeeee*. I get to spend all day chilling out with Aimee on lifeguard duty, and then we're going to go get ready for the big Casa Nadar summer beach party tonight. (Joe is on shift for it, because Belinda said he is "one of the only lifeguards she actually trusts". I'd be offended but it's fair enough, really). So, I get to party without having to worry about any *boys*. Or *kissing*. Or even *accidental arm brushing*. I don't have to worry about a bloated food baby in my bikini or whether I've got spinach in my teeth. I don't have to worry if my make-up is running down my face from sweat. I don't have to worry about eating too many sausages on a stick and someone trying to hold my hand whilst I've got sausagey fingers. I just get to hang out with my friends! *What a luxury.*

I put on my Hawaiian flower necklace and dance downstairs, where Dad is making eggs.

"You're in a good mood," Dad comments.

"I got dumped!" I cry, twirling around the kitchen. "*Three times!* Well, four actually, if you count Freddie."

"Ooo-kay." Dad shakes his head and mutters something

about never being able to understand teenage girls. He stirs the eggs. "Want some? They're cheese and chives."

I smile, thinking of Joe. Those are his favourite eggs. "Yes please!"

After breakfast I skip off to Casa Nadar, where Aimee is waiting in the lifeguard chairs with a glass of orange juice outstretched.

"Orange juice?" I ask. "What happened to virgin coladas out of a coconut? Or refreshing coolers out of melons?"

"I know, right! How will I ever drink out of a glass again and enjoy it?" She holds the glass of orange juice out in front of her and scowls at it. "It's so mundane, so . . . *uninspired!*"

"Why don't you go get something else then?"

She lowers her sunglasses and peers at me over the top of them. "You think *this*. . ." She points at the glass of juice. "Is by *choice?!* I asked for my regular, M, and Noah said. . ." This is the first time I've heard Aimee refer to Noah as "Noah" rather than "Hot Sauce". "He said *I would have to pay for it.*"

I squint at Aimee in the sunlight. She's *actually* got tears in her eyes.

"Well, isn't that normal?"

"No, Maya. One of those virgin colada smoothies costs about an hour's wage. I don't toil here all day for nothing.

How did you think I was drinking so many of them? Noah was obviously giving them to me on the house."

When she says it, it makes total sense. Otherwise Aimee probably would have bankrupted herself. But now that I think about it, I'm not sure *I* ever got a free smoothie from Noah. . . Did I? Before I can sift through my memories, Aimee continues ranting.

"You've properly mugged him off, Maya. And now your friends are paying the price." She sniffs.

"*WHAT?!*" I splutter with disbelief. "*YOU* told me to get to know all of them!"

"Did I?" Aimee pops her sunglasses back on and leans back in her chair. "*No*. . . No, I think I always leant towards Noah. Piercing eyes and free drinks is obviously the way." She sighs deeply. It has a different sound than her previous sighs. Faraway, like she's truly troubled about something. I think about asking, but maybe it's best not to press her in this mood. It probably is just the lack of free smoothies.

"Well, I'm *so sorry* my abominable love life has left you paying for things and drinking out of glasses along with the rest of us mere mortals."

"Apology accepted." She lifts the juice in a fake cheers. "At least my tan is looking on point."

I open my mouth.

"And *don't* start talking about melanocytes," she adds.

"I wasn't going to." *I was.* She might as well say "my skin damage is looking on point". I pull a bottle of factor fifty out of my bag and start lathering it on, just for good measure.

Despite our unfortunate beverage limitations (juicegate), Aimee and I end up having the *best day ever.* We just talk rubbish and laugh and soak up the sun. (Well, Aimee soaks up the sun; I observe the sun from beneath appropriately shady protection).

"If you weren't going to be a doctor, which you definitely are, but for argument's sake . . . what would you be?" Aimee asks, as she paints her toenails a bright green in preparation for tonight's party.

"Um. . . Something else sciencey, I guess. I've always liked space."

"Ugh!" Aimee cries. "You always take everything so seriously. I meant, if you weren't going to do what you're *obviously* going to do, what would be that weird random thing that you've always a little bit thought about doing? Cowgirl? Painter? Rapper?"

I think. My mind draws a blank. "Nope. I got nothing."

Aimee sighs. "All right, all right, fine. You're an astronaut. Would you snog an alien?"

I burst out laughing.

"I don't know. What does it look like?"

"It's a *hot* alien."

"Hot how?"

"It doesn't look human, obvs. It's, um, blue and it has one eye. But it's just *hot*."

"Do we get on?"

"I mean, it doesn't speak English. Or speak at all. It communicates via arm wiggles."

"Then how do I know it wants to snog me?"

"It wiggles its arms enthusiastically?! I don't know, M, there's just *vibes* between you and this alien, all right. Would you snog it?"

"Sure. I mean, if nothing else I'd definitely make history, right? First scientist to snog an alien. That's pretty impressive."

We determine that if I were to snog this alien, kids would probably be learning about my top scientific research for centuries to come. We also determine that if Aimee wasn't going to be a video game designer, she'd be one of the ballroom dancers on a dance reality TV show (I comment that her interpretive "parsley dance" would probably set the world on fire). Or, she says she would at least make the costumes for them.

"Speaking of, what are you wearing to the party tonight?" Aimee asks.

"I dunno, top and shorts? I thought it was just a beach party?"

Aimee shakes her head. "Sorry, M. Belinda's enforcing a *dress code*." She pulls a crumpled leaflet from her pocket. On one side is a picture of a tall cocktail glass, on the other is a blow-up floating sunlounger. It's *very* Belinda.

Casa Nadar is opening its doors for...

THE BIG LUAU BONANZA

Please join us on the 15th August at 7.30 p.m. onwards for:

Pool competitions including...

Volleyball

Chicken

Blind man's bluff

For those on dry land, party games including...

Limbo

Weight lifting

Pass the post-it

NB: NOTE STRICT "SMART AND SWIMWEAR" DRESS CODE.
Entry to any wearing shorts, joggers, trainers or any items considered to be generally "slouchy" will be strictly prohibited.

"*Smart and swimwear,*" I repeat. "What does that even mean?"

"It means you're either in a glamorous dress or you're half naked," says Aimee. "I'm coming in my green dress and wearing my bikini under it in case I want a swim."

"Very wise." I nod, trying to rack my brains for what I can wear. I think I've got an old, black halter-neck dress of Mum's hanging around at the back of my wardrobe, and a pair of her heels.

When we finish our shift, I wait for Aimee to get changed and look around for Joe. He might be arriving soon. Aimee sees me glancing around the pool.

"I think you're safe, M," she remarks. "Adam's halfway around the world by now, Noah's shift finished ages ago and Jake's probably at Lydia's pre-party party."

"Lydia's having a pre-party party?" I ask.

"Obvs, our invitations got lost in the mail." Aimee winks.

"I wasn't looking for any of them anyway," I say. "I just thought Joe might be here."

"Ah." Aimee goes strangely quiet and absorbs herself in tying up her laces. Eventually she says, "I don't think his shift starts until the party does."

"Oh cool, shall we go get ready at his?" Then I

remember that's probably not an option. "Oh wait, we'd have to get changed with the door open. We might scar someone."

"Huh?" Aimee stands and picks up her bag.

"You know, Joe's gran's *open door* rule."

"We always shut the door." Aimee shrugs. "Otherwise the whole house would hear Joe crying like a little girl as I beat him."

"Oh," I say. "Weird. Maybe she was in a particularly traditional mood that day."

"Maybe." She bends back down to her laces yet again. If she ties them any more tightly she might cut off the circulation to her feet. "Let's go to yours, anyway," she suggests. "Please will you curl my hair?"

I *am* very good at curling hair. Aimee says it's my "steady surgeon's hand".

"Of course," I grin, and we head back to mine.

Aimee and I spend the entire evening bathing, shaving, waxing, perfuming, curling, straightening, spraying, painting, applying everything we can think of. Twice my Dad comes upstairs and heads immediately back down choking, yelling, "The fumes! The fumes! I've been poisoned!"

By the time we're finished, I look at myself in the

mirror and wonder if I should make an effort more often. I straightened my hair and even managed to get the flyaway bits under control. My mum's old black dress really suits me, probably because we have the same lanky figure. (My wrist support is finally off, thankfully, so it's not ruining my outfit.) I usually just wear make-up to make myself look less dead, but spending longer than five minutes on it has a very different effect.

"You look *banging*," says Aimee, checking me out in the mirror.

"Why thanks, so do you," I reply.

"You've got something in your teeth, though," she says.

"Oh, thanks for telling me. You're a good pal."

"I actually noticed it earlier. I was toying with the idea of getting you back for juicegate but I couldn't follow through."

We both burst out laughing. I've had so much fun just hanging out with Aimee today at the pool and getting ready. And after *all this effort*, now I can't wait to inevitably find Joe at the party and stand in a corner just the three of us, stuffing our faces with whatever snacks Belinda has laid out.

"Ready for tonight?" Aimee offers me her arm. "Will I do as your date?"

"Don't get me wrong," I reply. "Three hot guys effectively dropping from the sky and all asking me out the day after I got dumped was kind of insane. But the best times I've had all summer were just hanging out with you and Joe. It feels so good to have all my eggs back and my head facing strictly forwards. *No more drama*."

At that very moment, like I've said a magic word and the fates have cackled their response, my phone buzzes.

Three times.

Three times?

My phone has only ever buzzed three times in a row once before. I pick it up cautiously, like it's a bomb that might go off, and wince at the screen.

Hey Maya. I'm just checking to see if you got my message from yesterday? I don't know what Lydia told you, but I'd like to clear up a few things. I'm coming to the luau party tonight so I hope we can have a chat. Jake x

Hey sook. Got halfway to the airport and changed my mind. I'll see you at the luau party. Adam

Hi Maya – I just wanted to say I really hope you

**didn't take "Proper Melt" in the wrong way!
I was just playing it back and I realize how it
must have sounded. Can we talk tonight? N x**

Aimee peers at my phone over my shoulder. "What was that about no drama?" She winks.

I stare at her, horror-struck. All my relaxation and poise evaporates in seconds. I can't believe that just moments ago I was thrilled with the idea of a chilled-out night, looking "banging" in my dress, and now I'm nothing more than a bag of nerves. My limbs seem to have *actually frozen*. Even if I wanted to go to the party now, I'm not sure how I'll get there. Aimee's probably going to have to pick me up and carry me.

CHAPTER

SIXTEEN

Aimee doesn't carry me, but she does drag me. When we arrive at Casa Nadar I'm glad she did. It's been *transformed*. It already looked amazing before, but this evening it looks stunning. There are fairy lights hung all around and their reflections twinkle in the pool. A DJ has set up in the corner, rather than just the usual speakers, and music is vibrating through the floor. Everyone being dressed up in formal wear lends the place an air of glamour it doesn't have during the day. Bright, white smiles flash and tans glow in the moonlight.

As I look around the place in awe, I get yet another flutter of butterflies in my stomach. I'm still anxious, but I can't deny there is something intoxicating about the thought of tonight's numerous possibilities.

"Hey, look! There's Joe!" Aimee waves.

Joe's face breaks out into a wide grin as he spots us. Seeing him makes me feel better instantly. We push through the crowds towards him.

"Hey!" Aimee hollers as we approach him.

"Hey! Er ... hey." He seems to notice what we're wearing and start coughing. "Er ... you look ... yeah. Nice. Not that you don't always look nice. You both look lovely all of the time. But tonight you look ... yeah. Is that a new dress, Maya?"

"It's my mum's," I answer.

"Oh, well, it's ... yeah," he says.

"And I see you are the only attendee to have got away without Belinda's smart dress code." Aimee gestures to Joe's lifeguard uniform.

"Yeah, I brought a suit with me though. She said I can switch with one of the others in a few hours."

Aimee whistles. "Oi-oi. Joe in a *suit*."

Joe owns a suit? First Joe has skin, now he's got a suit, I think. Then I wish I hadn't, because I'm reminded *yet again* of what's underneath the suit. Will the image ever stop plaguing me?! Joe smiles at Aimee's teasing and I look beside me, pretending to be distracted by a table.

The three of us hang out for a bit, being highly

antisocial, just as I predicted. We grab a huge bowl of Mini Cheddars and sit it on Joe's lifeguard chair, people-watching and people-mocking. There are so many people here I wonder if I'll even see Jake, Adam or Noah at all. They could easily go unnoticed amongst the crowds...

Famous last words.

I am mid Mini Cheddar number sixteen, mid thumb-war round two with Joe. I'm just relaxing, thinking this will probably be how the rest of the evening will go, when a familiar voice echoes across the crowds through the speakers. The music is switched off and everyone abruptly stops talking.

"Aha, thanks so much, buddy," says the loud, booming voice into the microphone, presumably to the DJ. "I really owe you one."

My whole body freezes. I look at Aimee in wide-eyed fear. She looks back at me with pure glee.

"Is that ... Hot Sauce?" she whispers. We both peer over in the direction of the voice. It's hard to see over the crowds so Aimee climbs up Joe's chair and puts her hand over her forehead like a sailor. She spots what she's looking for in the distance and rubs her hands together in satisfaction.

I take it that it *is* Hot Sauce.

"Oh my God." Aimee starts flapping her arms about.

She puts one hand on Joe's shoulder and one hand on mine and shakes us both. "Oh my God, he's got his guitar. Maya's about to get *serenaded*. It's like an *actual teen movie*."

Aimee is enjoying this *way too much*. I'm still frozen in shock. I'm not quite sure if I'm excited or mortified, or both. No ... just mortified, I think. I look across at Joe, who gives me a small, grim smile then looks down at his shoes. If I didn't know him better I'd say he looked ... sad? But knowing Joe as I do, I think he's probably just getting sentimental. Joe cries at the end of every single romcom, let alone when they happen IRL.

Oh my Days. Is this *actually happening IRL?!*

"So," Noah says. He clears his throat. "Sorry for this interruption, guys. I promise we'll have the music back in no time. But first, I was hoping I could play you all a song. I hope you don't mind."

Aimee reaches for my hand and drags me up the ladder of the chair, so we're both standing on it. I can see Noah now. He's wearing a suit (*damn*) and has a guitar strapped across his body. He holds his guitar steady in one hand and the mic in the other. Every now and again he jerks his head to flick his fringe.

"*We do mind!*" I hear Belinda screeching from a far corner, attempting to get to Noah.

"What's she got her knickers in such a twist for?!" exclaims Aimee. "Someone needs to tell her a party's not a party without a public serenade."

Belinda doesn't manage to push her way through the crowd in time to stop him. She shouts some other far less polite things but they get drowned out as Noah carries on talking.

"I originally wrote this song because I was dealing with some difficult feelings for a girl, who didn't seem to notice me in the way I noticed her."

The crowd *awws*. Even Belinda slows down her pursuit of the microphone.

"But then I realized, why should she notice me if I wasn't prepared to express how I was feeling? To find real love you've got to *be* real, and I was playing games. So this one's called Proper Melt, Point 2."

He plays a few notes on his guitar. I can genuinely feel the collective swoon from every girl in the room. He takes a deep breath and starts to sing.

"Proper melt;
I was too proud to become one;
Proper melt;
Even for the perfect someone;
Proper melt, proper melt, proper melt;

Now it's time to be real;
Proper melt, proper melt, proper melt;
Take a breath and let yourself feel;
Proper melt..."

The soft guitar notes drift through the audience on the summer breeze. He sings the rest of the song to a completely captivated crowd. At the end of the song he says, "Thanks, that was for... Well, I think you know who you are." He hands the mic back to the DJ, gives a quick wave and disappears into the crowd (who are all cheering *wildly*).

Oh my days. I feel completely overwhelmed.

Aimee is jumping up and down. "Oh my God, M!!! That was AMAZING! When he gets famous can I be a backing dancer? And then steal the show and get famous myself, obvs."

"I..."

"What are you thinking?" She suddenly stops bouncing on her toes. "I guess it's got to be Noah now, right?"

"I..."

"I mean, a public, cringeworthy serenade and two songs written about you. He must really like you."

A fleeting expression crosses Aimee's face then. I'm not sure, but I think she looks slightly ... disappointed?

But I must be imagining it. She was so caught up in the thrill of the drama a few moments ago, and hardly anything bothers Aimee.

I've barely had time to gather my thoughts or let the song sink in, when there is a shriek. Someone points to the high dive, the bottom of which Belinda has cordoned off with red tape. All heads at the party turn up to the sky. There is a figure climbing up the ladder in the dark.

A very toned, burly figure.

"HEY, SOOK!" Adam shouts when he reaches the top. "DID YOU MISS ME?"

"DO NOT JUMP!" Belinda's voice screeches from ground level. "DO YOU HEAR ME? DO NOT JUMP!"

I actually feel sorry for Belinda. She's only just finished dealing with one disaster and now another strikes. She probably spent ages making sure this party went off without a hitch.

"DO NOT. . ." she repeats, rushing towards the ladder.

Too late.

Adam launches himself off the diving board into a series of big, complicated flips. His body twirls around against the stars until he finally lands with a gigantic SPLASH!

Everyone gasps. Water sprays all over the people standing around the edge of the pool ... including Belinda. She stands in open-mouthed horror, but no one else seems to mind. Everyone who's been drenched in water cheers. They start taking their dresses and suits off and jumping in the pool.

"YEAH!" Aimee shouts, throwing her dress off and running after them. I look on in horror. I guess it's kind of sweet, but this is *so embarrassing.* I like order ... and structure...This evening is turning into *pure chaos,* and it's all my fault!

"I guess the swimwear part of the evening is starting early," I half-say, half-sigh to Joe, watching Aimee dive elegantly into the pool and start splashing water at a group of random boys.

"I guess it is," he mutters.

Why does Joe sound so flustered? I know why *I'm* flustered, but Joe's not the one responsible for a real-life public serenade and a real-life mass jumping-into-a-pool!

Just then I hear a little bark and a squeak. A gold, fluffy head on four tiny legs pushes its way through the crowds towards me.

"Hi, Stefan." I bend down. "What are you—"

The sound of Taylor Swift's "You Need To Calm Down" starts booming through the sound system.

Suddenly Stefan freezes. Then he stands on his two hind legs.

No. Please. *No no no.* Not another attention-seeking stunt. I don't think my heart can take it! I'm going to have cardiac arrest, age sixteen, when the average age for it is *sixty!*

In time with the music, Stefan shuffles to the right, and to the left, then he puts all four paws back on the ground and shuffles around in a circle. He stands up, shuffles to the left, and to the right, and down again in a circle.

By this point, all I really want to happen is the ground to swallow me up. (But OH MY DAYS HE IS SO CUTE.)

Everyone who can see Stefan has stopped what they're doing, mesmerized by the fluffy dancing creature before them. A circle has formed around him. Lots of people are taking videos on their phones and cooing. I can hear a lot of "Is that the most adorable thing you have ever seen?" and I hear one girl say, "Do you think we can teach our dog to dance to Summer of Cyanide?"

After a minute or so Stefan finishes his routine and dips into a deep bow at my feet.

Argghhhhh but *awwwww.*

"Hey! Well done, Stefan," I say weakly. "You mastered the bow!"

He looks up from my feet and I notice a little note tied to his collar, with "Maya" written on it. I untie it and unfold the paper.

Hi Maya. Jake didn't want to disturb the party TOO much because cousin Belinda might be upset, but he's hoping this is cute enough to compete with a serenade and a fancy dive.
Love, Stefan

It definitely was.

Jake emerges from behind me and Stefan runs towards him. "Well done, Stefan!" He leans down and gives him a high five, which is gently returned with a little fluffy paw. (*My HEART.*)

"Maya," Jake says. "I don't know what Lydia told you, but . . . we never officially got back together."

What?!?! But Lydia said. . . I'm totally taken aback! Before I can say anything, I see Adam, dripping and wrapped in a towel, clearing a path through the crowds towards us. He approaches us.

"All right, Maya," he says. "How's it going?"

"Erm, welcome back from the shortest trip ever?"

I say. I'm not even sure how my brain is managing to connect to my mouth to form words, at this point.

Adam shrugs. "I thought it would taste like freedom, but it turns out there's nothing free about being an Instagram model. All this 'wear this, stand here, do that'. All before we even got on the plane! I'd much rather spend the summer here, chilling with you."

Then I notice Noah skulking around the edge of the pool, guitar strapped to his back, looking in our direction.

Before he can say anything, Joe, who is still standing next to me, starts talking in my ear. "Look, Maya, you're busy," he mutters. "I'm just gonna leave you to it."

But he's interrupted by Aimee. She comes running towards us calling, "MAYA! MAYA!"

She's wearing a giant, blow-up duck around her middle, so getting to us looks like quite a challenge. It occurs to me she would have made life easier for herself by taking the duck off first, but that's not Aimee's style. Everyone she pushes past glares at her. She doesn't seem to notice.

When she finally reaches me I'm still so distracted by the duck I barely hear what she's saying. She's talking very fast and banging on about "being the bearer of bad news".

"Woah, woah, Aimee, slow down," Joe says.

"I don't want to give you more drama, M." Aimee bites her lip.

"I think we're past that point." I sigh, my head spinning. What could possibly be *more* dramatic than a serenade, a high dive and a dancing dog?

"Empty Box is here." Aimee finally spits it out.

"Huh?" I massage my temples.

"Freddie. Freddie's here."

SEVENTEEN

Freddie's here. *Freddie's here.*

All right. OK. All right.

Freddie's here.

I look at Aimee and Joe, watching me with concerned eyes, and wish yet again that this really had been a drama-free night with my friends. I look at the three totally gorgeous, totally lovely boys standing in front of me and ... I don't know. Wouldn't I be more thrilled by all of these romantic gestures if I *really* liked these guys? Rather than just feeling panicked? Being forced into a spotlight is my worst nightmare, sure, but if I had genuine feelings for any or all of them, wouldn't I be feeling at least *a little bit* more excited?

It was so sweet of each of them. I really liked Noah's

music, but . . . I think I was more awed by his performance skills than by the thought of our potential relationship. Adam's dive was super impressive but I think I'm more excited about his body than I am about the thought of being together. And Jake, he's so sweet, but . . . when he was making his grand gesture, I can't help but think my heart was melting more for the dog than for him.

They're all *perfect*. And they all *want me*. I still can't quite believe it. And I can't quite believe that I'm not feeling more. But in this moment I just can't lie to myself. I'm not. I can't help but think that even on our dates I was more swept up in the *idea* of what was happening, rather than what was *actually* happening.

I feel so deflated. The last few weeks have been a farce. With a sinking heart, I realize I must be feeling this way because deep down I wanted Freddie all along, and now he's back. Familiar Freddie, who's funny and popular and exactly the right height and has weirdly perfect elbows and eats all his peas and needs an adorable amount of help organizing himself. I'd thought I was getting over it, but clearly I wasn't. My heart feels like it's going to fly out of my chest at the thought of seeing him, dwarfing any feelings that I've had for the three boys standing in front of me.

Aimee puts her arm around me. Or as close as she

can get, with the rubber duck between us. "Sorry, boys," she says to Jake, Adam and Noah. "I've got to talk to Maya about something. She'll catch up with you later."

Adam, Jake and Noah nod dutifully and rejoin the party. Once they're gone Aimee puts both her hands on my shoulders. "He's looking for you, M. Do you want me to tell him to bog off? Because I will get rid of him *so fast*. . ."

"It's OK," I squeak. "I should talk to him. Thanks, Aimee."

"Do you want me to lurk behind you? Make sure you're all right?"

"You look incredibly threatening with that giant inflatable duck around your middle," I smirk. "But I'm OK." I square my shoulders, taking on a warrior stance. The thought of finally confronting Freddie after all this time makes me nauseous, but I feel ready.

She squeezes my shoulders in response and stands back. "I'll wait for you right here."

Joe clears his throat. "I mean, I'll be. . . Not that I. . . Freddie is. . ." He finally gives up on whatever it is that he's trying to say. "I'll be here too," he finally concludes.

"Thanks, guys." I give them a small smile.

I head off through the crowd. Most people have taken off their "smart wear" now. Looks like it's officially the swimwear portion of the evening. One group have already started dancing in the corner by the DJ. The limbo contest is reaching the final round. Two girls are left in and the pole is *ridiculously* low. Surely it is *physically impossible* to bend backwards that low?! The core body strength one would have to have to achieve that level of balance is insane. But I'm getting distracted. I need to plan what I'm going to say to Freddie.

Oh my days. What *am* I going to say to Freddie? My mind's gone blank. I must still like him, because I'm having such an intense reaction to his return, but do I want to tell him that?! He did pie me over text. Maybe I should just tell him off, and take some time to properly get over him? No dating, just Jaffa cakes, as I'd originally planned?

I carry on past the pool where the game of chicken has started. I'm oddly pleased to see Belinda joining in the games. She looks like she's having the time of her life as she cavorts around on the back of some fit guy. Good for her. She deserves to have fun tonight. She organized the whole bloody thing. She may not be my favourite person but you can't deny she gets things done.

Then I spot Freddie and my heart lurches into my mouth. He's playing chicken with Lydia on his back. She's screaming with laughter as he charges through the water, pretending like he might throw her off. Every muscle in my body tenses up. A giant knot appears in my stomach and my breathing becomes shallow. I think of my little adrenal glands, sitting on top of my kidneys, releasing a surge of adrenaline, increasing my heart rate, blood pressure and energy supplies.

I forgot how nervous Freddie makes me. Even after months of going out I would feel tongue-tied around him, always afraid of saying the wrong thing. It's funny, but I didn't feel half so relaxed going out with Freddie after three months than I did going out with Noah, Jake or Adam for three days. I guess that must be what it's supposed to feel like when you really like someone.

I stand at the edge of the pool like a pure lemon for a few minutes, waiting for Freddie to notice me. I had felt super confident in my dress earlier, but now it feels all wrong on me. I keep pulling at the straps to adjust it and wishing it weren't quite so tight. A few minutes later he looks up and sees me.

He flashes his standard, cheesy Freddie grin at me. I'm not sure why but it's not the reaction I was expecting. A *grin?!* After the last thing he said to me was "I'm not sure where my head's at", after taking another girl on holiday instead of me, after not speaking for weeks...

But then, Freddie's never serious. I remember

that was what I liked about him. I thought it would complement me because I take things *very seriously* at all times.

He puts down Lydia, who glances in my direction without acknowledging me and leaps on to the shoulders of another half-naked boy. You have to admire her confidence. If it were me I'm sure I'd miss and end up kneeing him in the back. Or if I did make it, the boy would turn to me and say, "Who are you? Please unmount me this instant, strange girl." Which I would understand and graciously accept.

In all the time I've been playing out this awkward scenario, Freddie has nearly reached me. I'm so nervous I can't even crack a smile at his Spongebob swimming trunks. He slicks his wet fringe back off his face and stops a few feet in front of me.

Ah. I remember now how perfectly matched his height is for me. Just a bit taller than me, but not so tall I am craning my neck towards the sky, like with Adam.

"I'm glad you found me," he says. "I was looking for you."

It crosses my mind that he can't have been looking *very hard* given that I was standing a few metres away and he was absorbed in running around with Lydia on his back.

"Yes," I reply. "Aimee told me."

"You look fit," he comments.

"Thank you." I pull at my dress again. Then I point at his trunks. "Spongebob."

Damn. Why can I never form proper sentences around him?! Sometimes there was the odd moment where Adam, Noah and Jake made me forget my own name, sure, but later on I was able to converse normally. Again, I suppose really liking someone means you're never truly at ease?

"Uh-huh." Freddie smiles. There are the dimples. Reason number two on the Freddie is Perfect list. "So can I pull you for a chat?"

"Yes," I say. I really wish some words except "yes", "thank you" and "Spongebob" would spring to mind, but those appear to be the three I've got to choose from.

We say nothing else as we head to the expanse of grass behind the pool, where there are fewer people milling around. We find a quiet spot behind a tree and stand dumbly for a second. It occurs to me how ridiculous we look, with me in a formal dress and him in a pair of Spongebob swimming trunks.

Eventually, as ever, my need to avoid awkward social interactions takes over and I search for something to say. "Did you enjoy your holiday?" I ask politely.

Why?!?!?! OMD, I HAVE to stop asking that!!!

"Ouch." Freddie puts his hands on his chest like I've shot him. "Cold, Maya."

I say nothing. I was being completely sincere, but pretending like I was being sarcastic and unforgiving is probably better than coming across as so pathetic I ask after the holiday I was uninvited from.

"It wasn't all that," he says. "It was crap, actually. It rained a lot so we had to stay indoors half the time. Lydia was moody as hell."

Ha! I think with satisfaction about the freakishly perfect weather we've been having at home, and all of the fun I've been having with Joe and Aimee, but then I feel mean.

"...And I missed you."

He missed me? *Really?!*

"Look, I know neither of us really knew where our heads were at. Lydia told me you were seeing her ex?"

"I..." I think about pointing out that this was *after* he broke up with me but he's already moved on.

"But I think it was all just a big misunderstanding. And I know what I want, now. I really want to be with you. My head's not going to get turned again. Shall we just put this behind us and get back on track, yeah?"

I open my mouth to disagree. *Was* it all a big

misunderstanding? He seems to be implying, again, that I had some share in causing our break-up. But then if he's suggesting I was at fault, how can he be so sure I want him now? My brain feels like soup. As ever with Freddie, he's so assured in what he thinks and the way he puts it across that I find myself doubting my own opinion. Maybe it *was* all a big misunderstanding, after all.

It's strange... A few weeks ago, I would have given anything for Freddie to realize he wanted to be with me. Because Freddie is what I always wanted, isn't he? He's got tons of friends, he's always the centre of the crowd in a way I could never be, he has everyone in hysterics, he's smart when he focuses ... When he's in the spotlight of popularity I enjoy basking in the glow and when I help him I feel needed. That's what makes us work, right? We complement each other?

I mean... Muscle-bound, wave-riding backpackers... Edgy, elusive musicians... Sensitive, kitten-rescuing aspiring vets... The last few weeks I've been living in a hormone-fuelled haze. They're all ridiculously, bonkersly, couldn't-have-made-it-up dreamy. But they're not *my* dream. Freddie is.

Right?

I should be over the moon. Freddie's words should be leaving me ecstatic, not confused. So why am I feeling so. . . I don't know. Like I still don't know where my head's at. I shake my head, trying to clear away thoughts of perfect dates with dreamy boys, sun-soaked hours spent laughing by the pool with Joe and Aimee – all of which are feeling less real by the second. This is real, I tell myself, Freddie in front of me, asking me to be with him.

"Maya?" Freddie nudges me.

"Yeah," I answer. "Yeah." My voice sounds faraway.

"Yeah, like. . . We can make it official again?"

"Yeah," I agree. "Yes, of course." I don't really think about what I'm saying. The words come out on autopilot, which I suppose is what happens when things are meant to be.

I'm back with Freddie. The Freddie. Perfect Freddie. Dream Freddie. My Type Freddie. Finally. It's what I've dreamed about for months. But I thought I'd feel different. . . I thought I'd feel happier. But I'm probably just feeling guilty and awkward because I'm now going to have to tell Adam, Jake and Noah that I was stringing all of them along. Once I've had a chance to talk to them, and once the dust has settled, I'll probably be thrilled. Right?

"YES!" Freddie lunges forward and picks me up. He's wet from the pool and I can feel water soaking into my dress. I remember how much Freddie liked to pick me up or rustle my hair. It should be endearing. But when he puts me down all I can think about is how he's left a big, wet patch on my dress. "BUZZING! Maya, that's so great. Come on, let's head back to the party."

When we get back to the party he kisses me on the cheek and heads off in the direction of the pool, where his mates are still playing chicken. It would have been nice to catch up for a bit longer, then maybe I could shake off these confused feelings, but maybe he's just super excited to tell his friends the good news.

Aimee and Joe are waiting for me by the edge of the grass. At first I don't recognize Joe. He's got changed into his suit and is pulling at the sleeves. He's tidied up his hair. He looks ... *so* different. I think briefly of the group of girls who giggle and stare at him in the gym. I can see exactly why.

Aimee is tapping her foot impatiently. "WELL?" She shouts at me. "Did you tell him to go pie himself?!"

I open my mouth. Is that what Aimee thought I would do?

"I ... no." I shake my head.

"All right, I know you're too polite for that. How did you put it? Did you tell him to dip his fork into a pie?"

"No," I say. "No, it was all a misunderstanding."

"A misunderstanding?" Aimee blinks.

"Yeah, both our heads were turned. But now both our heads are facing firmly towards each other."

"What?!" Aimee shrieks. "You ... *what?!* That is SUCH a load of—"

Joe puts his hand on Aimee's shoulder. "Ames."

"No, I'm sorry. You're not really telling me after this whole summer dating boys who literally fell from the heavens, gracing us mere mortals with their chiselled cheekbones and unattainable abs, you're back together with Empty Box?"

"Ames, if Maya's happy..." Joe continues.

Aimee folds her arms and casts her eyes up and down me. "She doesn't look happy to me. She looks soggy and miserable. And so do you, Joe."

I blink. Huh? Why would *Joe* be miserable?

"Aimee..." Joe's voice is stern. I don't think I've ever heard Joe stern before. "*Don't.*"

Aimee sighs.

"I'm going to get a drink. Hopefully from a watermelon." Now Joe just sounds flat. I've never heard him sound so unenthused about drinking from a watermelon. He walks off without making eye contact.

What is going on?!

"What's that about? Is something going on between you two?" I ask.

Aimee still has her arms crossed. "I've said it before and I'll say it again, M, for someone with such high grades and militant levels of organization, you're not the brightest."

OMD. What did I miss?! I had always wondered if Joe might like Aimee. Is it possible I've been so involved in daredevil assault courses and moonlit gigs and dancing puppies this summer that I failed to notice that she liked him back? For some reason the thought makes me feel like I'm going to vomit.

"I do need to talk to you about something," she says.

And with those nine words, despite *everything else that's happened*, for the first time tonight I feel like my whole world might be about to change.

CHAPTER

EIGHTEEN

Aimee stares at me for a long moment. She looks *guilty*. Like that time she told me I ate all my Jaffa Cakes, then I caught her eating the last one. But worse. "I like Hot Sauce," she finally says.

And just like that, my world shifts back into place. I breathe out.

"*Noah?*" I clarify.

She bites her lip and nods.

"*You* like *Noah?*" I cannot compute this. My outspoken, ridiculous and quite frankly lazy best mate likes quiet, pensive and ambitious Noah?

"Yes," Aimee confirms.

"You don't like Joe?" I say again, just to make sure.

"*Nothing is going on between me and Joe, M.*" Aimee

continues, rolling her eyes. "We are friends, always have been friends, always will be friends. You and I are more likely to start going out than me and Joe." I feel an instant, inexplicable sense of relief. What's that about?! Am I *that* terrified of being left out in our threesome? But Aimee and Joe wouldn't do that to me. I know in my heart, with complete confidence, neither of them would ever have let me feel like a third wheel. So why was I *so* bothered at the thought of them together?

"...likes me back." Aimee is still talking. "And I wasn't even going to mention it, because you've been out with him, but now you're back together with Freddie I figured you might be OK with it? But if you aren't, I one-hundred per cent will not go there. Even if you are dating Freddie now. If you find it weird in any way then whatever, it's not worth it."

"He likes you back?" I ask.

"Uhhh, yeah. There is no non-awkward way to tell you this, but... Noah was actually serenading me."

I blink. Aimee is grimacing like she's waiting for me to start crying.

I *burst out laughing*.

"OH MY DAYS!" I choke through my laughs.

Aimee hesitates, as if checking I've not lost it, but when she sees I'm actually OK she starts laughing too.

We both laugh and laugh and laugh and end up bending over, gripping each other.

I wipe a tear from my eye. "I cannot *believe* I was standing there all earnest and worrying how I was going to handle his feelings, and he wasn't even singing to me."

It all starts to fall into place. Noah never actually said "Maya" in his song. He said, "You know who you are."

"*Oh*," I say. "So was his original song about you?"

"Uh-huh." Aimee nods. "Apparently he kept making me ALL THE FREE DRINKS to get my attention and I didn't even notice he existed. When he stopped making them for me I thought he was moody about you. But like, of course I didn't notice him, I thought he was into my friend."

"*OH*," I say again. "Did he ever want to go out with me?!"

"Uh, well." Aimee's eyes move awkwardly to one side. "Apparently when we walked back to your house that time he was trying to ask me out and I just kept going on about what a huge SoC fan *you* were. . ."

I snort. That's hilarious. "Oh, Aimee." Then I feel a warmth spread through my stomach. That is so Aimee, to be so confident a guy should like me, she completely misses that he likes her.

She winces. "I know. And then he had loads of fun at

the gig with you, but he was worried you got the wrong impression because you danced. I think he just really likes dancing. And he gets overexcited when SoC plays." She sighs. "He's just so passionate. . ."

I raise one eyebrow. Her eyes are all faraway and her voice is soft. She looks all . . . melty.

"Aimee," I say. "Have you become a *proper melt?*"

She snorts. "I think I have. I know it's not like me. And I know it seems like an odd match. But I don't know. There's just something about never really knowing what he's thinking. It just makes me want to know. And I'm so direct, I just ask him outright, and he says he likes that." She shrugs. "It helps him to, I quote, *open up. . .*"

"Well," I say, "of course you must go for it. Be proper melts together. Become his muse. Etc. etc. etc."

"Are you *sure?!*" Her eyes are large and pleading. "Because you know there's nothing in the world that is worth risking even a *tiny, minuscule, imperceptible* rift between us for."

This moment makes me think back to my chat with Lydia and how she was basically asking me the same thing about Jake, as Aimee is about Noah. Except she wasn't. It seems so obvious to me now. Pretending to ask someone if they mind about something that you have every intention of doing anyway, just to assuage your own conscience, is not being a true friend. Aimee is genuinely asking me if I mind, and I know with absolute certainty that if I did mind it would have an impact on her actions. Comparing the two conversations I suddenly realize that maybe Aimee was right about Lydia... Maybe she's not as nice as I thought she was, after all.

Aimee is, though. She is literally the best person on the planet. In terms of friendship baskets, I'd put all my eggs in hers and know they were in the right place.

"I know. I'm positive," I assure her. "I wish I was this sure about my own love life."

"Well, we're agreed on that, M." Aimee nods. "Look, you need to talk to Hot Plate and Hot Dog. And..." She looks like she's about to say something else, but then she says, "And maybe that's enough for one night."

We hug and she makes her way back into the party to find Noah, and I go to find Adam and Jake. She's right. I need to let them down once and for all. I've finally gathered all my eggs together and put them in one basket. Freddie's basket. The basket I wanted all along.

I find Adam first. He's easy to spot because he's right in the middle of the weightlifting competition. Instead of just using the weights set out, he's holding them *and* some guy from the audience is sitting on his outstretched arm.

"Three ... two ... one!" The umpire declares. "WE HAVE A WINNER!"

The bemused guy hops down from Adam's arm and Adam bows. The umpire holds his hand in the air and the crowd whoops and whistles. Oh, to be so strong that people would cheer at me for merely holding things in the air.

Once Adam's done soaking up his glory, I edge over to the crowd and cough loudly. Adam sees me standing there.

"Sook!" He beams. "You found me. Let's go for that chinwag."

My chest is tight from the thought of rejecting him. He's so lovely! I run through all the ways I can phrase it to make it sound nicer, as we head over to the fake beach area and sit on a sunlounger. Someone with a drinks tray offers us some sort of colourful smoothie and I grab one. I take a big, huge gulp, so that I have a second longer to avoid this *hideously awkward social interaction*.

"Adam," I say. "You are awesome. You are fun, and easy-going, and ... erm ... very attractive. I have had SUCH A GOOD TIME with you this summer..."

"Maya, Maya." Adam lays a giant hand on my shoulder. "It's OK, really. You don't need to let me down gently. I saw the way you were looking at that guy. You looked like you were having a right laugh."

233

I did? Was it *that* obvious I still liked Freddie this whole time? And I'm not sure I'd say chatting about why he dumped me by text and took another girl on holiday was a laugh *per se*. . .

"I had loads of fun with you too," Adam continues. "But it's all good. *Que sera, sera*. You should crack on with him."

"But I feel *so bad*." I take another gulp of smoothie. "You left your trip."

"Ah, I woulda left anyway. I don't think a career as a model is the one for me. But hey, look, I've just found out I get a cash prize for this weightlifting thing! If I add that to my savings from teaching all summer, that's more than enough for a flight to Hawaii!"

Relief washes over me. *He's fine. We're OK. He doesn't think I'm a gigantic snake.* I don't know why I'm so surprised. Adam seems to take most things on the chin.

"Hawaii?" I smile. I think he'd mentioned that was the number one spot for surfers.

"Yeah, I'm not quite good enough to surf there yet, but if I train up a bit I bet I can ride that perfect crest."

"That's great, Adam." I point to the flower necklace he's donning. "And we already know you'll fit right in at a luau."

He laughs. "Right, well, I bet you'll wanna get back

234

to your bloke and your crazy best mate with the duck. I'll be seeing you."

We hug one last time. (Am I sure I'm sure about this? Those arms. You'd feel *so safe, Maya...*) I wave goodbye as he clears a path through the crowd with ease and disappears off into the night.

One down. One to go.

I thought I might feel less nervous after chatting with Adam, but I feel just as on edge thinking about having the same conversation with Jake.

I find Jake by the DJ, dancing with Stefan. A circle has formed around them. Everyone is cooing over Stefan shuffling to the left and then to the right, even though he must have done it a hundred times by now.

Nope. There I go. I'm cooing too. It *never stops being adorable.*

When Stefan sees me he starts barking and runs towards me. Jake follows him, giving me a small wave. I try to smile but I'm so apprehensive my face is frozen, so it probably looks more like a grimace.

"Maya." He goes in for a big, warm hug, before we move to the side of the dance floor. "How are you? Are you all right? You seemed distressed earlier."

Bless Jake. Even though I'm the one who's been keeping her options open with three different guys, he's still asking about how *I'm* feeling. Although he might care less once he realizes I've now made it official with a fourth guy none of them even knew anything about. Gulp. How muggy does that sound? Maybe, if I don't end up becoming a doctor, I should be one of those people who dresses up as a giant mug and stands outside coffee shops.

"Yeah..." I start. *Where is the smoothie guy? I need another awkward smoothie to hide behind*! "I, uh, listen, you're *so lovely*. Like, one of the sweetest, and smartest, people I've ever met. But... I realized I still have feelings for someone else."

Jake's lip wobbles. Is he going to cry? *Please don't cry.* I don't know what to do when other people cry. Once Aimee couldn't stop sobbing about a bad exam result that she'd studied really hard for, and I pointed out that emotional crying could release oxytocin and endorphins so she'd probably feel loads better soon.

She didn't.

"Are you OK?" I put my hand on Jake's shoulder. Stefan has sensed Jake's upset as well and nuzzles against his foot.

"Yeah, fine." Jake sniffs. "Honestly, it's not you. I mean, obviously I'm disappointed you don't want to see where things go, but this whole thing has made me realize I'm not properly over my ex yet, either."

"Oh," I say. "Lydia?"

Jake nods.

I'm confused. If he still likes Lydia, why doesn't he go get Lydia? "Well, it seems like she really wants to get back together..." I suggest.

Jake shrugs. "Yeah, only because Belinda told her about us. I don't know, I just feel like every time I start getting over it, it's like this little alarm bell goes off in her head and she clicks her fingers, and I go running back every time like a *proper mug*."

"You're not a mug, Jake," I say.

"Not any more." He wipes the corner of his eye. "I don't want to be with someone just because they're jealous I'm moving on, you know? If she really wanted to be with me she wouldn't have messed me around so much."

I nod. "That's totally understandable."

"I think I need to be on my own for a bit longer," Jake resolves. "Next time I meet someone like you I'll be properly ready." He nudges my shoulder.

I grin.

"Hey, Maya," he continues. "Maybe this isn't my place, but... Don't make the same mistakes I did, yeah? I mean, your ex wanting to get back with you on the same night three guys publicly try to impress you. He might be

237

genuine, I don't know the guy." He shrugs. "But just be careful. You're a very trusting person."

"Oh." That's the only thing I can think of to say. I suddenly feel a bit dizzy. I realize from the outside it might *appear* as if that's exactly what Freddie's done. It might *appear* highly suspicious to someone who didn't know him. But I do know Freddie and there were lots of good qualities that attracted me to him in the first place. I *definitely remember* his capacity to always hand in his homework on time without fail (unlike Aimee, cough) was on the Freddie-is-Perfect list. Those are the actions of a reliable, trustworthy person. I trust him. Don't I?

"Sorry, I'm an idiot." Jake must have noticed how taken aback I was by his comment. "What do I know? I'm probably just being overly sensitive because of my own situation. I saw you guys earlier and you looked really close."

Did we? That's the second time someone has said something nice about me and Freddie together this evening. I guess we must really make a great couple, like I always thought.

Jake hugs me and disappears off into the party, Stefan close at his heels.

Done.

Sorted.

Phew.

That was fine. Noah liked Aimee all along, Adam is sailing merrily off to travel the world again and Jake needs more time to get over Lydia anyway. For all my unintentional mugginess, I'm relieved to find that I haven't ended up mugging anyone off.

I sit down on a patch of grass, watching the party. Jake's dancing with Stefan again. Adam's teaching a group of girls how to stand properly on a surfboard. Aimee's got her rubber duck back on and is teaching Noah some sort of duck-themed dance. They're certainly doing a lot of waddling, anyway. (She got intense, dry Noah to waddle in public? He must *really* like her.) I see Freddie dancing with Lydia in the crowd. They're not exactly dancing like Aimee and Noah, more like . . . swaying and looking pristine. But they look like they're having a great time in a different way.

I briefly wonder where Joe's gone. I hope he's having a good time. I'm sure he is. I'm sure he's on watermelon cooler number fifteen and getting loads of compliments on his suit.

Looks like everyone else is living their best life, so I can be free to live mine. I can be happy about Freddie now. Except . . . *am* I happy? I thought it would feel so much better than this. So much lighter to be carrying one basket instead of three. So why don't I *feel* lighter? Why do I feel like I've replaced three baskets for one great big, *giant* basket made out of lead?

CHAPTER

nineTEEN

As the party goes on, I finally decide to take charge rather than sitting here like a lemon. I get up and make my way over to where Freddie and Lydia are dancing. It's possible that it's just taking time to get used to being back on with Freddie. Of course it's going to feel strange … it's only been about half an hour and we haven't even spent any of that time together. Maybe I just need to commit more. Spend some time with him and remember all the things I liked about him in the first place.

As I move towards the dance floor, I see a familiar back walking out the door. *There's* Joe. My heart fills with joy at the sight of him. Or maybe I could just dance with Joe for a bit instead… I run after him.

"Joe!" I yell.

He turns to face me reluctantly, without saying a word. He looks upset.

"Are you going home?" I ask. "Don't go home! Stay!"

"Nah, I've had enough."

"What? No!" I say. It's funny, but even though I've barely spent any time with Joe all evening, I'm desperate that he doesn't leave. I know the party won't be the same without him.

Joe gives me a sad smile. "Why do you want me to stay, Maya? Is there some dance you would like me to teach you to show Freddie? Or maybe a swimming technique? Or a magic trick? I'm sorry, I don't know any magic tricks and I can't dance and ... I'm an average swimmer. I think I've run out of ways that I can be useful. And even if I could, I think I'm done helping you impress other guys."

What? Is Joe being ... *sassy*? What is he on about?!

"Huh?" Is all I can think to say. I'm so completely confused.

"I guess I could take it with three mega dream hunks who seemingly fell from the sky purely to make me feel inferior. Because at the end of the day they all actually seemed like nice guys. I could do it if you were going to be happy. And don't get me wrong, I'm OK with having little to no self respect if it's the right thing for you, but

I have to draw a line somewhere. I just can't do it for Freddie, I'm sorry."

Again, *what?!*

"Huh?" I say again.

"I can't, I'm sorry, Maya. I don't think Freddie's a good person." He shrugs.

Joe's annoyed at me. That much I think I understand. And he doesn't like Freddie. But . . . is he implying I only want to spend time with him when I'm using him to help me impress random guys?! That is so *mind-blowingly incorrect*. I am quite insulted a friend would think that of me.

"Joe, I don't want you to help me with anything," I defend myself indignantly. "I just want to spend time with you."

Joe sighs. He looks at his shoes and fiddles with the sleeve of his suit. "Sorry, Maya. I tried to stay and have a good time, but I think I just want to go home."

He looks so *sad*. It's heartbreaking. Why is he having such a bad evening? I can't let a pal go home like this. He can't have got all dressed up in his suit just to go home after an hour. "If you're really not going to stay, I'll come with you," I say. "We can play Mario Kart."

As soon as I say it I know it's exactly what I want to do anyway. None of the rest of the party matters. None of the drinks or the dresses or the games or the people matter if Joe is at home alone feeling sad.

"It's all right, don't take pity on me," he says.

"I'm not. . . I *want* to come with you," I assert. I feel myself getting a bit teary with frustration. Why is he being like this? Why doesn't he believe that I'd rather be with him than at this stupid party?

"You and Freddie have just made it official." Joe puts air quotation marks around the last three words. "You should probably spend time with him. I'll see you tomorrow." He hesitates, then gives me a quick hug. As he pulls away from me I already miss him. I watch him walk down the street with a pang. From behind, in his suit, I almost wouldn't recognize him.

I head back to the dance floor feeling completely deflated. Aimee sees me, stops waddling and waves. Noah waves too. I must look tragic because she shouts, "What's wrong?" immediately. As I get nearer she says, "Oh, did Joe leave?"

I frown. "Yes, how did you know?"

"He said he was going to earlier. I tried to get him to stay, but. . ." She shrugs. "You know Joe. Parties aren't his favourite thing at the best of times."

"What's up with him?" I ask.

Aimee rolls her eyes. "I've said it before and I'll

say it again, M, for someone with such high grades. . ." Mid-sentence, she is distracted by a conga line forming. People are putting their hands on the shoulders of the person in front of them and starting to move around the pool, kicking their legs out to the side. "GUYS!" Aimee frantically beckons me and Noah forwards. "COME ON!"

After that conversation with Joe, I am seriously not *in the mood to conga*. I have never been less in the mood to conga. If there even is such a mood. I watch Aimee and Noah conga away into the night.

I see that Freddie and Lydia are also not congaing. They're sitting on a sunlounger by the side of the dance floor with a load of their other mates who are too cool to conga.

I head towards him and feel that familiar sweating of palms, raised pulse and shortness of breath. My adrenal glands have always worked *incredibly hard* around Freddie.

I sit down next to him and his group of friends. He puts his arm around me. Lydia smiles at me, I *think* genuinely. I watch her turn away from me with a flick of her hair and make some joke, being the centre of attention as usual, and decide that maybe she's not what me or Aimee thought. She's not an especially kind person or a nasty one. She can be friendly enough and I'm sure she never meant to hurt my feelings, or Jake's, she's just a bit oblivious and self-absorbed.

"How's it going?" Freddie's breath is hot on my ear.

"Not so great," I admit. "Joe just went home. I think he's upset about something. I think I might have upset him."

Freddie squeezes my shoulders. "He'll be all right. Just relax and enjoy the party. You'll make it up tomorrow."

Then he continues talking to his mates.

Is that . . . it?

I guess it wasn't a bad response. Just kind of *meh*. I think of how concerned Joe seemed about me earlier, even the two guys I was dumping, compared to me genuinely telling Freddie I'm bothered about something . . . and him saying "it will be fine" and carrying on messing around with his friends.

I sit there quietly for a few minutes. We haven't even seen each other in weeks. Surely he should want to talk to me more. But instead he's telling an anecdote about how this guy in his class did a really loud fart in the middle of an exam. All his mates are laughing. Lydia's rolling her eyes but giggling. She says, "Freddie, what are you like, that's *so* gross."

I try to muster a smile, but I can't. I never understand

why people find the release of intestinal gases as a result of digesting food endlessly hilarious. But Freddie's *funny*, isn't he?! That was one of the things I liked about him back when we first met. I think of all the fun I had this summer, with the guys – with Aimee and Joe – and I try to remember all the times Freddie made me laugh.

It's at that moment I have a shocking realization. . . *I can't find any.* I have a lot of memories of standing around whilst he made all his *mates* laugh. But I don't think *I* was laughing.

I stand up, pushing myself out from under Freddie's arm.

"You all right? Where you going?" Freddie asks.

"I need a drink," I lie.

"OK." He nods and goes back to talking to his friends.

I hasten towards the café area. I feel awful. Worse than when I was feeling guilty for dating three guys at once. I can't help this nagging sensation that I might have made a mistake. Is that possible?! I was *so sure* about Freddie. . . I look back on all the time I spent obsessing over him. OK, so he's not that thoughtful and he's not as funny as I thought. . . But there are lots of other things I like about him, right?! And OK, so he doesn't seem *that* interested in having an actual conversation with me after weeks apart, but maybe he's acting so normal because this is just how it's supposed to be. Me and Freddie together. Maybe it doesn't need to be a big deal.

I shake myself and head back over. Not a big deal... Not a big deal... Normal... Normal... As I approach the group again, I hear Freddie's voice, loud and clear on the summer breeze.

"Naaaah, she *begged* to have me back, mate. She said none of those guys had anything on me."

A group of male voices laugh. I freeze and my heart stills. Is he talking about *me?*

"Are you *sure* that's what she said, Freddie?" Lydia's voice. She's teasing him. "Because I saw that Australian guy when he was swimming and WOW."

"All right, Lyds." Freddie sounds aggressive now. "Yeah, that's what she said. She was practically on her knees. Even pleaded to do my homework again."

More loud, male laughter.

I ... *begged* ... to have him back?

I *pleaded* to do his homework?!

I'm rooted to the spot. I wait for the effect of his words to hit. I'm ready for the tears to come. But nothing happens. Has he hurt me so much that I've gone numb?

I can't believe it ... and yet the sad thing is, I can. I can completely believe it. Having time away from him this summer, I must have been slowly piecing it together. . . That he's not the person I thought he was. In one way I'm heartbroken to hear him talking about me like this, and yet nothing in me is surprised.

I stumble back to the café area, sit down and take some deep breaths. *Where is Aimee?!* Ugh, she's probably still having fun with Noah in the pool. I don't want to ruin her evening. She's been listening to me angsting all summer. She deserves one night off.

I've been trying to push Joe out of my mind, but now that I'm alone I can't help but think about him at home on his own. Is he OK? What's he doing right now? Is he watching TV with his gran? Or a movie with his sisters? Maybe in his room playing video games on his own? I think of the beanbag chair next to his that I'd give anything to be sitting in right now.

Sitting alone, I start to feel more and more upset. Not because I'm upset about realizing my "relationship" with Freddie is over, but because I don't know how I can have *missed this*. All this time. *All this time*. I thought he liked me, but it turns out I'm just a joke to him, to entertain his friends. I thought we were a team, but apparently I'm just an easy ticket to a zero-effort A-star. Everyone was right to be suspicious, and I was the idiot. He was just back with me so that he didn't lose face when I ended up with someone hotter or more charming than him.

I lay my head on the counter and breathe in and out, thinking of my diaphragm contracting, increasing the space in my chest cavity for my lungs to fill. I think of the oxygen traveling through my bloodstream to make energy in my cells.

I sense someone sit down next to me and put their hand on my back. At first I'm filled with relief that Aimee has found me, but when I sit up I find myself face to face with Belinda.

Belinda. Has *her hand on my back.*

Does she think I'm someone else?! Someone who didn't lose her a netball match or walk in on her filling her bra with synthetic substances? Or is she putting her hand on my back as a threat rather than a sign of comfort?

"Are you OK?" she asks. Is she recording me so that I admit something embarrassing and she can blackmail me?

"Uh. . ." I'm not sure how to respond. I'm still finding it difficult to breathe.

"Look, Maya." She leans back in her chair and takes her hand off my shoulder. "I'm . . . *sorry*. . ." She forms her mouth around the word like she's biting into a lemon. "If I've been a bit *harsh*. But my cousin's a sensitive soul and I'm not a fan of people who take advantage. I don't want to see him getting mugged off."

I open my mouth, instantly distracted from Freddie. "I wasn't. . ."

"I know." She puts her hands up. "But you have to admit, running around Casa Nadar all summer with three different guys laying it on factor fifty, you can understand why I was concerned."

I nod. I *do* understand. If only she could have seen how anxious the whole experience made me.

"But after talking to Jake I realize I had it wrong. He just told me about everything that's happened between him and Lydia and I had no idea."

She seems sincere. I don't *think* it's a trick. . . I think Belinda is *actually being nice to me*. Maybe she's finally forgiven me for the netball incident?!

"I still haven't forgiven you for the netball incident," she carries on. "I'm never going to get over how someone so intelligent didn't even bother looking up the rules before stepping on to my court. But you treated my cousin with respect so, I just wanted to check you were all right. I overheard Freddie and Lydia talking and I figured that's why you were over here." She gestures to my slumped arms, as if to say "why you were over here deep-breathing on the counter".

Belinda puts her hand back on my shoulder. "Take it from someone older and wiser, Maya." (She's only two years older, but she's being kind, so I'll let it slide.) "Forget about him. He's *such* a douche."

I study her face, which is screwed up in anger. She's genuinely raging on my behalf, about this muggy guy she doesn't even know. We have *nothing else* in common . . . but it feels nice to be united in this. And as she says the words "forget about him", I realize that . . . I sort of already have.

I think I've been slowly forgetting about him all summer.

"Are you OK?" Belinda asks when I don't respond.

I think about her question and realize that yes, *I am OK*.

I am *completely fine!*

"You know what . . . yes, Belinda," I laugh. "I think I actually am."

I don't think I'm numbing myself to any pain. I really don't. I feel like I've just dropped my giant basket made out of lead and set all my eggs free.

"Thank you, Belinda," I say, springing out of my chair. "And thank you for talking to me about things that others may have found far too intensely awkward."

"Never been a problem for me." She winks.

I'm not sure why but I find myself throwing my arms around her. I think I'm giddy from all my free-floating eggs. "Belinda, you have excellent breasts, with or without enhancers," I say.

Her eyes widen. I think she might be about to laugh but I'm not sure. Before she can say anything I run off into the crowd. I know what I have to do.

CHAPTER

TWENTY

The party's starting to slow down now. The games have finished and people are putting their clothes back on and starting to trickle out the gates. I've not got much time to find Freddie.

Everything's becoming crystal clear as I rush around looking for him. I think of all the time I spent focusing on stupid things like Freddie's height and dimples and well-proportioned elbows and love of greens. All the moments I convinced myself that Freddie caring more about telling jokes than paying me attention was fine because I hate being in the spotlight anyway. That helping him with his schoolwork made sense because a disorganized person needs someone to organize them. I mean, that only works if the other person is bringing something to the table as well. Whilst I was convincing myself I found his jokes funny and helping him study . . . what did he do for *me?!*

I just can't believe I made such a classic, scientific error! I'm always so careful, and analytical, and measured! And in some ways the data said we should fit . . . but the result was *breathtakingly wrong.* I was so desperate to get the answer I wanted that I ignored too much other evidence. Breaking up with me over text, can't even be bothered to reply to me and then invites his mate on holiday instead of me. . . *That's* what I should have been paying attention to. I can't believe how long I spent going over such stupid, meaningless boxes. None of that stuff actually matters in finding the right person for you!

Freddie only wants me now because other people want me. He never really wanted me at all and I'm not sure I ever *really* wanted him. On paper he was lots of things that sounded great, sure, but what good is it going out with the funniest person who doesn't make *you* laugh? Or the most popular person if all it means is they've got more time for everyone else than for you?

He's still sitting in the same place as earlier. I run up to him.

"Hey, can I . . ." I pause. Well, everyone else says it, so why not? ". . . pull you for a chat?"

"Sure," he says uncertainly.

All his mates go, "Oooooooh!" and start nudging each other. Freddie flushes slightly and rolls his eyes at his friends, trying to pretend like it's nothing. We go and stand beneath the same tree that we "made it official" under earlier this evening.

"Freddie," I say. "This doesn't feel right any more. I'm not sure it was ever right. I don't think we should have gone back there."

It feels good to say it politely, but how it is. I don't want to be nasty, but I don't want to make apologies or excuses because I feel awkward either. Aimee would be *so proud* of me.

"What?" Freddie frowns. "But you said. . ."

"Well, you said we were going away together and then took Lydia, so I don't think I'm the worst culprit at changing my mind, do you?" I fold my arms.

I hear Aimee's voice in my head. "*WHO IS THIS SASS QUEEN AND WHERE HAS SHE BEEN HIDING?! Enjoy him melting under your vicious burn!*"

Freddie opens his mouth and closes it again. He looks hurt. But I know for sure now he's only hurt because of his ego, not because of me. "So which one of those muppets is it then?" he asks, I'm assuming referring to Jake, Noah and Adam.

"None of them." I shrug. "I just don't want to be with you."

If Freddie was flushed before, he's now a *deep shade of red*. It's weirdly satisfying thinking that I caused this widening of capillaries and blood travelling closer to the surface of his skin, given everything he's put me through.

That's the last thing I'm able to say to him before he snorts, muttering, "All right, whatever," and starts walking off.

OMD... I can't believe how right Aimee was. He is *so muggy*. I stand under the tree watching him retreat for a little while and can't believe how indifferent I feel, apart from a huge weight lifting off my shoulders. I don't even dislike him. He's just ... well, as Aimee said, an Empty Box.

I go to find Aimee. She's got changed back into her dress and is leaning against the gates. The sight of her standing waiting for me as the crowds slip out on to the street makes me smile.

"Did you have fun tonight?" I ask, as I approach her.

"I mean, I'm still sore about losing the limbo contest." She tilts her head to one side. "Turns out they don't accept crawling under the bar as a legitimate limbo technique. Oh my God, and Belinda CONFISCATED my duck! She said I was too immature to be trusted with it!"

"Too immature for a giant, bright yellow rubber duck." I shake my head. "That's a new low, Ames. Where's Noah?" I ask.

"Went home. He was feeling inspired so wanted to seize on it before, and I quote, *it evaporated like summer rain.*"

"My. He *was* feeling inspired." I laugh.

Aimee pulls a bit of hair over her face like a long fringe, in imitation of Noah. "I don't write the music, Aimee, the music writes me. When it calls I must listen." She bursts out laughing. "I never saw myself with a serious arty type but OH MY GOD, turns out it really does it for me."

We both cackle. I think about how silly the "type" thing has turned out to be. After all the completely different, dreamy boys I've been out with this summer, and realizing the one person I thought was my ideal match isn't right for me at all, I have no clue what my "type" is any more.

"And where's Freddie?" There's a shift in her tone as she asks this.

"We broke up," I answer tentatively.

Aimee balls one hand up into a fist and smacks it into her other palm. "Where is he?" she growls. "I cannot *believe* he did this again after – what was it this time – two hours?! That's a new record. Oh, Empty Box, when

I find you..."

"Ames, Ames." I put my hands up. "It was me. I broke up with him."

"OH." She unfurls her fists. "Why? What happened?"

"You were right about him all along," I admit. "He's... Well, I'm sure he'll make someone very happy, but it's not me."

Aimee takes a moment as she computes this, until her face breaks into a wide, dazzling grin. "Well that's ... *great*, M," she says. Then she starts moving her arms forward and to the side in parallel.

"What are you...?" I begin.

Then she starts moving her arms to the right, as if she is chucking something on to the floor. She repeats the motion three times and starts giggling to herself.

"I call this dance 'Empty Box, Get In The Bin'." She keeps dancing. "I've been saving it for the day you dumped Freddie. What do you think?"

I watch her again and see that the dance is basically her miming putting a box in the bin.

"I think... Are you sure you want to go into video game design *before* trying your luck as a dancer? You've really got the moves."

Aimee stops dancing and does a little bow. "All right, let's go home you," she says. "My Single Pringle."

We start walking along with everyone else leaving the party. Even though everyone looked amazing at the start of the night, with perfect hair and make-up, I'm enjoying everyone's end-of-night appearance too. Everywhere I look, girls are loping home with their heels in one hand, wet hair, smudged eyeliner, faded lipstick and wrinkled dresses.

As we make our way down the street, away from the fading noise of Casa Nadar, I raise my head towards the stars and find myself thinking about one person. And it's not any of my three dreamy dates and it's *definitely not* Freddie.

The idea started to form when both Jake and Adam commented on "some guy" who I looked like I was having fun with, and looked comfortable with... At first I assumed they meant Freddie, but now I look back, my conversations with Freddie were all behind a big tree. There's no way they would have seen me. There's only one person they could be talking about and ... now that I think about it, that person unexpectedly makes way more sense.

In this moment I finally understand what Noah meant in his song "Proper Melt". When Aimee asked me who out of Noah, Jake and Adam made me feel "soft, sappy and silly", I couldn't choose, but now I realize that's not the sort of question you should have to think about to know the answer.

I think about Joe and my heart opens up like the night sky I'm staring up at. And not in the way my heart opens up for Aimee, or for Noah, Jake or Adam, or for anybody else.

"Aimee..." I say softly. "I think, I think maybe I've been an idiot."

"Well, yes, Maya," she replies. "We've established that. But Freddie is history now, so..."

"No, I mean, about something else." I take a deep breath. "Aimee, do you know why Joe was so upset earlier?"

Aimee sighs. She stops walking and turns to me. "I think you know the answer to that, M. But my question is, why are you asking? Because if you have ... *certain feelings* ... I want to tell you. But if you don't I think it's best we leave it alone."

I take another deep breath. "I ... I think my head's been turned without knowing it."

"How can you be facing something and not know it?" Aimee grills me.

"I don't know... I have a second, secret head?"

Aimee is quiet for a moment. She looks deep in thought. Finally, she says, "They say love is blind. Maybe that should be love is your blind, secret second head."

Even though she is being deadly serious, I can't help but laugh. "You've been spending too much time with Noah," I say.

"Seriously, M." She puts her hands on my shoulders. "I know I said to *keep your options open* and *see where it goes* with Hot Dog and Hot Plate and Hot Whatever ... but this isn't like that. If you actually— oh my God, I can't believe I'm saying this. If you actually *like Joe* then you've got to mean it. No messing around."

As soon as she says it out loud, that I "like Joe", I realize that's exactly how I feel. I realize just how much I like Joe.

OMD. I LIKE JOE.

I. LIKE. JOE.

JOE.

"*M*," Aimee repeats. "Do you mean it?"

I nod. I do. I really, *really* do. It must have been coming on so slowly that I'm not sure when I started to mean it. I think back on all the ridiculously movie-worthy dates I've been on this summer, with boys that seemed like they quite literally walked out of the pages of a girls' magazine. I had an amazing time climbing huge walls, going to glamorous, secret gigs, eating fancy meals ... but I think I had a more amazing time *before* the dates. Jumping through hula hoops in the locker rooms at Casa

Nadar, listening to music in my bedroom practising our stupid "brooding looks", throwing mushrooms at each other in my kitchen and playing stupid outdated board games, sitting on Joe's ridiculously comfy beanbag chairs whilst he smashes me at Mario Kart. *Those* were the best times of my summer.

"I mean it, Aimee," I say finally, and know that I do. "I really mean it. But do you think he likes *me*? I don't want to presume..."

Aimee raises one eyebrow. "M, the boy's been like a lovesick puppy for months. I always knew he liked you, but you were so obsessed with Freddie. And then when all those FIT GUYS dropped out of the sky... I don't think I've ever seen someone so crestfallen. But pleased for you, too, obviously, because he wants you to be happy. And Freddie was definitely *not* making you happy."

"I always thought he liked *you*." I shake my head at how I can have got everything *so wrong*. I am a *woman of science!*

"Because he can actually look me in the eye? Yeah, I can see how you got confused, but no."

"I like him, Ames," I say. "I think I *really like him*."

Aimee shrugs. "Well, if that's how you feel then you're walking in the wrong direction." She turns me back down the street, towards Joe's house.

CHAPTER

TWENTY-ONE

I look at Aimee. She looks at me. Is she really suggesting I go *charging round* to Joe's house to declare my love for him? *Right now?* Without thinking it through or planning what on earth I'm going to say?

"Aimee, that's bonkers. I'm not heading around to Joe's house in the middle of the night."

"It's ten p.m.," she says flatly.

Is it? I look at my phone. She's right. Damn Belinda for having a party that started in the afternoon!

"I can't... I don't... What do I say?!"

"Don't overthink it," Aimee assures me. "Just go. He's probably sitting there crying into his game controller about you getting back with Freddie. It will be a nice surprise."

"What if it isn't?" I start panicking. "What if he's

given up on me? He seemed so annoyed at me earlier. He implied I'd been using him. What if he's so sick of all my muggery that he can't forgive me? What if he *pies me?!*"

Aimee shrugs. "Better to find out now rather than later."

OMD. Up until now I hadn't considered that Joe pieing me was a *real possibility*. Now Aimee hasn't dismissed my worry it's risen tenfold.

"I . . . I can't. . ." I stutter. "I can't do it."

"Oh my God!" Aimee yells. "JUST GO!"

She stands in the middle of the street and spreads her legs and arms, blocking my path. She points behind me.

I could, obviously, push past her. She is not an impenetrable fortress. But she's been so right about everything else so far, namely Freddie, that maybe I should actually start listening to her.

"All right," I say. "I'm going, I'm going!"

"GOOD LUCK!" she shouts, still in her weird starfish position.

She stands there watching me walk all the way down the street. Every so often I glance back and she makes shooing gestures with her hands. Finally, I turn a corner and she disappears from view.

Slowly, I begin the walk to Joe's house. I take baby steps along the street, breathing in the cool, late night summer breeze. Nothing can soothe my thudding heart as I play out how the conversation is going to go. How am I going to start it? What will he say? In the ten-minute walk I manage to run it through my mind a hundred different ways. In one he just points at his mug and closes the door. In another he gets an actual pie out of the fridge and smashes it in my face. In one I don't even say anything, he just leans in and kisses me as soon as he sees me. (KISSING JOE? Am I really thinking about *KISSING JOE?!* The thought almost makes me want to throw up. But not in a bad way.)

In one particularly strange scenario, he smashes the pie in my face and *then* kisses me, and then comments on the flavour of the pie. (Apple and blackberry, his fave.) It's then that I know I really do have to stop playing it out in my head and just go for it. Which is convenient, because I've reached his house.

I stare down the pathway at the front door. It suddenly occurs to me that I can't just go ringing the doorbell at ten p.m. What if his gran or his sisters are asleep? What time do eighty and eight year olds go to bed?

Thankfully, I see light filtering from under the closed curtains of the front room out into the garden. Someone is still up. I make my way up the path and knock softly on the front door.

I hear movement inside. Someone shuffles slowly through the hallway. The door cracks open and Joe's gran peeps her head out suspiciously. When she sees it's me her eyes light up.

"Oh, Maya!" she says. "Hello, gorgeous. I'm afraid Joe's gone out so you're stuck with me."

Joe's out.

Not a single one of my scenarios ended with "Joe's out". Where on earth is he?! He doesn't have many friends apart from me and Aimee and he's definitely not with Aimee. What if he met someone else at the party? Did I miss my chance already?! I suppose, what with him having watched me date ridiculously hot guys all summer, it would probably be exactly the karma I deserve.

Two little heads pop up at an upstairs window. And two normal-sized heads pop up at a downstairs window. Great, now Joe's mums and sisters are all watching. I *love* doing embarrassing things in front of an audience.

"Oh," is all I can think to say. "Well, I'm sorry to bother you, I'll just. . ."

"Oh, it's no bother. I'm not usually up at this time, but we had a little incident, a nightmare about those godawful yellow creatures they're so obsessed with, eating them alive." She gestures upstairs to Joe's sister's bedroom.

I smile. "Do you have any idea where he might be?" I ask.

"I thought he would be at yours. Have you tried Aimee?"

"Ah, yes, he's not there either. Never mind, I'll try tomorrow. Thanks, Annabelle."

I *think* I manage to cover my hopeless, spiraling disappointment.

"Oh, my love," she says. "You look so disappointed."

Or not.

"Have you two had a barney? He looked a tad upset earlier," she asks.

"Errr. Well ... yes, actually. I'm trying to find him to make it up to him. But I'm sure I'll find him eventually. Thanks anyway," I say again. "I'll see you soon!"

I start heading back down the path. She calls after me, "Yes, I'm sure I will! I always knew you two would get it together eventually."

I turn back and she winks, and shuts the door.

OMD. Did everyone else on the planet know about me and Joe before I did?!?!

I get my phone out, racking my brains for Joe's whereabouts. Then I remember, in all the new and unexpected things I have learned about Joe this summer, the one thing that might help me.

Joe's late-night swimming.

I start running back the way I came, back towards Casa Nadar.

As I approach I see Casa Nadar twinkling in the distance. The fairy lights are still on and casting the whole building in an ethereal glow. It looked beautiful earlier, but without the crowds cluttering the lawn it's breathtaking. It stands in peaceful silence against the stars and, not for the first time, I appreciate how lucky I am to have spent my summer here.

I walk slowly towards the gates and give them a slight nudge. Sure enough, they're open. Either Joe's here for his late-night swim or Belinda forgot to lock up after the party. I pray that it's the former as I open them with a slow creak and step inside.

Instantly, I hear the gentle splashes of someone gliding up and down the pool, and relief mixed with anticipation flows through me. I tread lightly along the path and take off my shoes to walk across the beach. The water ripples and sparkles in the moonlight and the sand is soft and warm between my toes. My whole body tingles as I get nearer.

When I reach the edge of the pool Joe is at the far end. He's stopped swimming, with his back to me and his head resting against the side. I almost call out, but

I'm suddenly so gripped with nerves that I perch on the edge of a sunlounger and wait for him to see me instead.

Finally, after what feels like an agonizing amount of time, he turns and launches himself off the back wall into a front crawl. When he reaches the other end of the pool, right by where I'm sitting, he finally notices me.

My heart is *hammering*. It's so loud and the air around us is so quiet that I wonder if he might hear it.

I'm expecting him to jump, or start choking on pool water, or yell something about me scaring him, but if he's shocked to see me he doesn't show it. We hold eye contact for a moment without saying anything, before he hauls himself out of the pool and moves wordlessly towards me.

I stand up. And try not to look too hard at his body, which is making my heart race even faster.

He approaches me and comes to a stop about a foot away. Even though he's the one who's wet and half-naked, I feel exposed. Everything I'm experiencing is so intense, like it's rushing in all at once having been hidden as it grew, slowly over time, and now it's grown so strong it's claiming all my attention. At this moment, I literally have space for nothing else in my brain but Joe. It's so overwhelming that it must show on my face, in my movements, in the air around me.

We stand for a few seconds. He still doesn't say

anything, and then I realize I'm the one who followed him here and invaded his privacy, so I'm probably the one who needs to speak.

"I'm sorry," I say. It comes out croaky, like I've forgotten how to use my voice.

"For what?" he asks.

"For not realizing. . ." I start, but I'm not sure how to go on.

"Ah." Joe runs a hand through his soaked hair. He looks past my shoulder as he talks. "Aimee finally outed me. It's all right, M, I don't need you to apologize. I'll get over it."

I was expecting him to ramble, but for once he's not. He seems surprisingly calm and sure of himself. Probably because he's already decided to move on. My heart sinks as I think *maybe he already has.*

"I don't want you to get over it," I squeak.

He looks at me, then. "What do you want?" he asks slowly.

"I want you to kiss me."

Now he looks surprised. He runs his hand through his hair again, as if thinking for a second, but he doesn't look away. Neither do I.

He leans in towards me and my pulse is racing, my palms are sweating, and I'm short of breath. But not in the way that I used to be around Freddie. These nerves are good nerves, nerves of anticipation, like my whole body is waking up to help me experience every bit of this moment to the fullest. And for once I don't analyse what biology is behind my heart is speeding up, or why my blood is pounding or what's causing the adrenaline rush, I just feel it. And when Joe's lips finally touch mine that's all I've got headspace for.

Joe is kissing me. I'm kissing Joe.

Joe has lips.

He's still wet from the pool and it soaks into my dress but I don't care. His hand cups my chin cautiously and then moves into my hair and on to my shoulder. The other one finds its way around my waist and pulls me closer.

Eventually we break away, breathless, and I take a big gulp of warm, summer air. That was ... yeah. I have *never* had a kiss like that before.

Joe seems lost for words and sits down on a sunlounger. I sit next to him.

"I really like you, Joe," I say. It now seems as clear as a summer's day. All my other worries have drifted off on the breeze.

"Are you sure, M?" He laughs. I love the sound of his laugh. "Because if I were you, I'd date Action Man Adam. I mean, he could probably kill me with his thumb."

"Don't get me wrong," I say. "Adam, Jake and Noah were all *dreamy*... And yeah, OK, Adam was super ripped and Jake was super sensitive and..."

I glance over and see Joe is wincing. This isn't coming out how I intended *at all*.

"What I'm *trying to say,* very ineloquently, is that I'm not sorry this summer happened. I enjoyed meeting so many different people and I had some experiences I never would have had if Aimee hadn't pushed me into them. But mostly, I'm grateful to have met them only because they made me realize ... they're not you. And yes, I could backpack across Asia or gig across Europe or do any number of exciting things, and that would be amazing, and we could do all those things, maybe we will ... but the point is I'd have just as good a time sitting at home with you and letting you crush me at Mario Kart."

Joe is silent for a moment. Then he says, "*Let* me crush you? Come on now, M."

We both burst out laughing.

"*Is that all you have to say?!*" I cry.

"No." Joe wipes a tear from his eye. "I've been wanting to say for ages, that if it were me, and *I* were taking you on a date, I'd take you to some science exhibition, with a backpack full of Jaffa cakes."

My eyes widen. "That sounds like the *best day ever.*"

My heart floods with joy at the thought of being with someone who knows me so well.

Joe puts his hand under my chin, tilts my head up and kisses me again. It feels so right. I can't believe I never thought about doing this before.

Now it's *all I can think about.*

"Joe," I say, in between kisses. "Do you want to make it official?"

"Ah." He kisses me. "Let's *see how it goes.*" Another kiss. "I'm *keeping my options open.*"

I thump him on the shoulder.

"Yes, Maya." He grins and touches his nose to my nose. "I would very much like to *make it official* with you."

Eventually, after lots more kissing, I say I should get home. Joe puts his clothes on and I watch him, feeling like one of those giggling girls at his gym. We walk out the gates of Casa Nadar, locking them behind us. While Joe turns the key I stare up at the building and across the pool, thinking once again about just how unexpected this summer has been. All these weeks I spent trying to work out my "type" and getting it *totally wrong.* I look at Joe and can't even think how I would describe him as a "type", he's just . . . a person. He's just Joe. Joe, my person.

EPILOGUE

Two weeks later, the summer is nearly over. Things have been progressively slowing down at Casa Nadar, until today, our very last day. With fewer people flocking to the pool, the afternoons have been longer and lazier, and thoughts of next year have started to intrude into our idyllic, sunlit bubble.

Aimee's last shift was this morning and mine and Joe's is now. We sit, side by side in our lifeguard chairs, looking across the pool and holding hands. Joe's thumb traces patterns across my palm and little waves of electricity shoot up my arm like ripples in the water. I can't believe that, only a month ago, I was playing thumb wars with this same hand without a second thought.

The last few weeks have been a blissful haze of laughter, kissing, Jaffa cakes and more kissing. We've been on some crazy dates of our own (we went go-karting with Aimee and Noah, and Joe made good on his promise to take me flamenco dancing – unfortunately Aimee was right, I'm not a secret natural, but it was still fun) but we've done some quiet stuff too. Hanging around at Casa Nadar consuming ice-cream and smoothies (once again free now Aimee's dating Noah), playing each other at video games, watching films with Joe's sisters and making dinner with my Dad. . . All of it has been equally amazing.

I'm feeling more emotional than I thought I would about Casa Nadar closing its doors for the summer. I don't want it to end. None of the staff do (I caught Belinda crying in the cupboard earlier, but this time instead of threatening me for catching her doing something embarrassing, she pressed me to her chest in a passionate hug.) But maybe we'll be back next year.

Belinda comes outside and taps her wrist. It's time to go. Joe gives my hand a squeeze and we climb down from our chairs. My heart fills with sunshine and I'm feeling, as I heard Belinda saying as she kissed goodbye to her favourite sunlounger, "totes emosh". But then Joe pecks me on the cheek, and he smells like lotion (factor fifty, as per my suggestion) and his hair serum and aftershave that have become so familiar to me over the past few weeks, and I know that everything I have loved most about Casa Nadar I'm taking with me.

We wave at Belinda, who waves back with a smile, and make our way across the decking one last time. Aimee's waiting for us at the gates with Noah. When she sees us she starts jumping up and down.

"GUYS!" she calls. "How emosh is this?! ADIOS, Casa Nadar! Thank you for all the fun times and the smoothies!" She blows kisses to the building.

Noah coughs. "Actually, I think it was me that made the smoothies," he says.

Aimee laughs. "Oh yeah, I guess you don't need Casa Nadar, do you?" she says. "Can you make me one when we get home?!"

Aimee and Noah start walking ahead, in the direction of Aimee's house, where we're all going to hang out and celebrate/reminisce. "Oh, God." Noah puts his head in his hands. "I shouldn't have said that. What have I started. . .?"

Joe and I follow behind them, and Joe takes my hand again as we walk down the street, Casa Nadar still glimmering white in the sunlight behind us. We smile at each other. I don't know what's to come, but I do know it's been an unforgettable summer.

ACKNOWLEDGEMENTS

As always, thank you to my mum. I wouldn't have made many a deadline without your unfailing support (practical and emotional!) The same goes for Patrick – you are the absolute best person ever. And a massive bev.

Hugs to all my pals for being such loyal babes – especially Nell who reads everything I write and champions it with aggressive enthusiasm (I'm going to pretend to publish an epic poem about socks one day and watch you push it on poor, unsuspecting colleagues) and Rachel for similarly packing off the Mackie clan with bundles of Seager books.

Props to Sophie Cashell for this genius book idea. I couldn't have imagined a project I was more eager to write. I've had the best time working on it with you – you are totally brilliant! And thank you to the whole team at Scholastic – Aimee for a gorgeous and spot-on cover,

Harriet for working so hard to champion the book, Pete for astute copy-edits (and gaming tips!), Lauren Fortune for always being wonderful, and everyone else working behind the scenes.

As ever, much love to the sort that is Lauren Gardner for being the most proactive and all-round fabulous agent. I wouldn't have half as much fun being represented by anyone else. And thank you to John and everyone else at BLM.

Last but not least, a big shout-out to the fellow funny teen writers whose chats and glasses of picpoul keep me sane.